Praise for *Found Time*

"*Found Time* hits the sweet spot between naughty and '90s-nostalgic. A sexy and sentimental read!"

—Robinne Lee, bestselling author of *The Idea of You*

"For those who lived through the '90s in downtown NYC, and those who only wish they had, this book is an utter delight."

—Kim France, author of *Girls of a Certain Age* Substack and founding editor of *Lucky* magazine

Found Time

CAROLINE GOLDSTEIN

831 STORIES

831 Stories

An imprint of Authors Equity
1123 Broadway, Suite 1008
New York, New York 10010

Cover design by C47
Book design by Scribe Inc.

Most Authors Equity books are available at a discount when purchased in quantity for sales promotions or corporate use. Special editions, which include personalized covers, excerpts, and corporate imprints, can be created when purchased in large quantities. For more information, please email info@authorsequity.com.

Library of Congress Control Number: 2025949097
Print ISBN 9798893311297
Ebook ISBN 9798893311303

Printed in the United States of America
First printing

www.831stories.com
www.authorsequity.com

For Jon

PART I

1993

1

"We're getting married," Nisha says as we walk to the Jeff Buckley show at Sin-é. I am uncomfortably aware of the crescent moons of sweat waxing at the armholes of my silk slip dress. This is the dumbest thing to wear in ninety-five-degree heat with one thousand percent humidity in the dead center of August, but I uncovered it at Screaming Mimi's for three dollars and made good on a promise to myself to wear things that look pretty but feel out of range. Trivial, sure, but maybe by taking small risks, I can somehow trick myself into becoming the person I want to be: free, embodied, and not so scared of the world. A little bit more like Nisha.

When I tried it on, I liked how the color of it, a sexy gunmetal gray, lifted the silver from my steel-blue eyes.

"I can't picture you in a wedding dress," I say now. I adjust my camera strap. It leaves a slick of sweat across my shoulder.

"That's because I won't be wearing a dress," Nisha responds. "I'll be wearing a bikini, as Jeff and I will be wed on the white-sand beaches of Bora Bora."

I laugh. "Your mother will be thrilled."

"She will be, actually. By that point, I will have discovered a cure for cancer, and that achievement will eclipse any questionable decisions I make thereafter."

"So we're going the biochemical engineering route today?"

Nisha grins. I don't know much about the singer-songwriter headlining tonight. But my best friend does. She's made it her mission to learn everything about him. He doesn't even have an album out but has already earned cult fame, in part through his appearances at the local spots—the Knitting Factory, Fez, Cornelia Street Café—and in part because he's the son of Tim Buckley, the folk-jazz musician who died of a heroin overdose at twenty-eight in 1975. Two years after Nisha and I were both born.

Nisha happened to sit next to Jeff at the SideWalk Cafe a couple of months ago, days after she and I moved into our apartment on Avenue A—a shoebox on the second floor of the building that also houses Two Boots, the pizza joint that effectively sustains us. And also, probably, the small colony of rats and cockroaches I once found peacefully coexisting underneath the warped floorboards of my bedroom.

When Nisha came home the afternoon of the Great Jeff Buckley Sighting, she told me that he drank his coffee black and smelled like cigarettes and peppers and rose soap.

She was sure she had fallen in love. Not that she worked up the courage to talk to him. He had the aura of an immortal, and she was merely a rising junior at NYU who didn't even know whether she wanted to major in biochemical engineering or physics.

As we round the corner onto St. Mark's, I accidentally kick a syringe. I watch it clatter into the street, where it's promptly run over by a bike messenger. No amount of NYPD officers, glossy condos, or newly opened Gap stores can buff the East Village to a shine.

We reach Sin-é, and my pace slows when I notice a limousine parked in front. A tendril of cigarette smoke curls out the driver's side window.

"I think your husband's going to be famous." I gesture to the car. It's so slick, just begging to be broken into. Only record-label people would be so arrogant as to bring it down here.

Nisha shrugs. "You don't think talented people deserve success?"

"Of course I do. I just don't think talented people need to sell out to do it."

She opens the café door for me. "Oh, my sweet, sheltered Lili. If only we could all be gifted artists with artistic parents. Life would be so much simpler."

"Simpler, maybe. But I'll never be able to afford the lavish lifestyle I truly crave," I joke. We both know I would happily subsist on cans of chickpeas for the rest of my life if it meant I could keep doing photography.

I gently push my way toward the stage, which is really just a few square feet of floor with a banner reading "Sin-é" hanging on the wall above it. Two years ago, I would have been trailing Nisha, but I'm trying to be bolder. Since the moment she came blazing into my room to introduce herself on move-in day of our freshman year, I knew I needed her kind of energy in my life. She was already glimmering then, and tonight, she is incandescent in her silver-foil minidress with a hot-pink bindi gleaming between her brows.

I've been to Sin-é once or twice, but never when the narrow, brick-walled room has been so full. It's mostly fellow NYU students, moonlighting actors, and some grizzled old Irish men, but over in the corner, at the table closest to the door, I spot two people, maybe in their midtwenties, locked in a conversation. Their heads are bowed over their steaming mugs—they famously don't serve hard liquor here, only tea, coffee, and cans of Rolling Rock—and the woman has a blood-red buzzcut and a slash of lipstick to match. She looks like a regular.

But the man is clean-cut, clad in a full suit despite the heat. Conspicuous among this sea of denim and facial hair. When he picks up his coffee cup, his watch flashes. He looks like a limousine rider.

All the tables are taken, the walls already lined with spectators, so Nisha and I have no choice but to sit on the floor, right in front of this duo. I shudder to think of dry-cleaning my dress, which will likely cost three times as much as the actual garment.

The toe of the man's dress shoe nudges my butt cheek. I feel my face burn. He quickly retracts his foot.

"Sorry," he mumbles. I pick up his scent, distinct even over the aroma of spilled beer that's soaked into the floorboards. Something piney. A sharp contrast to the sweltering day.

Nisha taps my knee and gestures to the stage. Jeff Buckley has appeared underneath the banner, his white Telecaster hanging across his chest. He's probably just come out of the bathroom, but it's like he conjured himself into being.

Now I understand what Nisha has been banging on about these past few months. This guy *glows*.

He steps in front of the mic and slings his guitar behind his back. He stomps his boot on the floor in a rhythmic beat. To someone offstage, he says, "Oh, you're rolling. Goodness. Is there any reverb to roll with?"

Then he begins punctuating his stomps with claps, and the song takes shape: Nina Simone's "Be My Husband." Nisha squeezes my knee in silent alarm. This is her favorite song, from her favorite Nina Simone album. This, the squeeze implies, is fate at work.

Jeff pulls his guitar around to play the second song, something I have never heard before but which evokes a familiar emotion: the irresistible melancholy of longing. Encountering this kind of sublimity is so overwhelming that it makes me want to capture it in an image. Discreetly, I take a single photo, the *click* of the shutter buried in the reverb. Then I abandon the camera and give myself over entirely to the moment. Over the course of the set, Jeff sometimes leans against the wall, like he's fiddling around in his own living room, casually being a genius. Sometimes he cradles his guitar closer to his chest, turning its face up so he can gaze upon it with more attention, as if it were a lover.

When the set ends, I look over at Nisha. Her face is streaked with tears.

"I think I just saw god," Nisha says.

For once—and just this once—Nisha is not overreacting.

"Go talk to him," I urge her. "Do it now, before he gets too famous."

At the front of the room, Jeff is already being swallowed up by the crowd. Nisha moves, zombie-like, into the fray.

I peel myself off the ground, unsticking my dress from the unswept floor. When I stand, my knees buckle underneath me. My legs have fallen asleep. *How much time just passed?*

"What'd you think?"

The guy in the suit. Over the past however long, I had been so fixated on the music, and the musician, that I'd almost forgotten he was just above me.

Earlier, I could tell that he was handsome, if out of place. Now I see that he's unbearably hot—and also, somehow, intensely familiar. As if I've previously seen the way his forearms flex under his rolled-up shirtsleeves, and already know how a section of his dark hair falls, curling over one eye. Like I'm familiar with how the corners of his mouth turn downward, not up, when he smiles, which makes it seem like he's harboring a secret I'm desperate to be in on. As though I've already heard the deep rumble of his laugh. And felt the weight of his body pressing me up against a wall.

It doesn't make sense. But to question it—I don't know where to start.

"I thought . . . I don't know what I thought," I say. "I have nothing to compare it to."

"In a good way or a bad way?" he asks.

For a moment, I wonder if I have the future of Jeff Buckley's career in my hands. "Definitely in a good way. I don't think he's signed yet, but if he's not, he should be."

"I agree."

I shift on my feet, still trying to get the blood moving in my legs. I touch the back of the man's chair for balance, accidentally brushing against his suit jacket, which he's folded and neatly draped over the back. His eyes shift to my fingers, then trail up my arm, my shoulder, my neck. I force myself to blink.

He nods at the red-haired girl. "You ready to go, Cat?"

"What time is it?" Cat runs her hand over her head.

He checks his watch. Up close, I see that it's a scuffed Timex. Not fancy after all. "Seven fifteen."

"Dinner's not until eight. Dad can wait."

Dad. My gaze darts between them.

"The express is running local," the guy says. "It'll take an hour to get up to Park."

"So you don't have a limo," I start. When they look at me blankly, I add, "So you can whisk Jeff Buckley away and offer him a million-dollar record deal? With a golden tablespoon of coke as a signing bonus?"

Cat cackles and elbows the guy. "I told you, you look like a fucking suit."

"Well, I am one, for the summer."

"Not record-label people, then." I feel foolish, out of sorts.

I look out the window. The limo is gone. So are the musician and his gear, I discover as I glance around the room. Patrons are slowly making their way out to the street, into the hot, real world.

I feel a flicker of panic. I'm not ready to go back out there. I'm not ready to face the impending school year—or the fact that I desperately need to get a job this semester after spending the summer doing nothing other than sunning myself in Tompkins Square Park and sneaking photographs of the leftover eighties punks, their mohawks drooping in the heat. I'm not ready to replace the feelings this night elicited with the avalanche of things I need to do.

"I'm definitely not cool enough to be a record-label person," the man says. "I have a temp gig at my uncle's investment firm."

"Which means he's basically working for free," Cat cuts in.

"I'm making enough to get myself this suit." He brushes his hands down his pant legs.

"My point exactly," Cat says. "Ten dollars an hour, Reid. I'd make more as a waitress at Veselka."

Reid. So the man has a name. A good one too.

"You're a waitress at Veselka?" I ask. If so, it would be a little like encountering East Village royalty.

"No." Cat smirks. "But I did fuck a line cook one time."

Reid laughs, then he turns back to me, his eyes studying

something. I'm suddenly very aware that I'm not wearing a bra, and that the hard peaks of my nipples are likely making this obvious to him as well.

He clears his throat. "I like your camera."

I fiddle with the strap. "Are you into photography?"

"Looking at it, sure. But I can't be the one doing it, assuming you want your head in the photo."

I try to fight a smile.

"Reid does write screenplays in secret, though. And they're actually not terrible." Cat arches her brows. I give Reid a glance that says, *Really?* and he returns one that says, *Up for debate.* "Which makes it even more of a shame that my dad has him identifying acquisition targets for IBM."

"I'm not actually identifying acquisition targets," Reid says to me, as if I know what those words mean. "I'm making photocopies and binding books out of research that other people did about identifying acquisition targets."

"Yes, but what beautiful binding skills you have." Cat grabs his chin between her thumb and her forefinger, giving it a squeeze. "My dad is no less immune to this *punim* than those girls are."

She motions to the table behind them. The two women sitting there look away quickly, caught.

"They've been staring at you this entire time," Cat stage-whispers.

Inexplicably, I feel a flare of jealousy.

That's when Nisha reappears, announcing her return with a forceful "*Lili!*" Her usual entrance.

"Did you get to talk to him?" I scan her face.

"He left with some people from Columbia Records," Nisha says. I exchange inside-joke glances with Cat and Reid. Reid's gaze lingers on mine.

"But guess what I got?" Nisha asks.

"His panties?" Cat quips.

"Almost better." Nisha waves a crumpled napkin in front of my face. "The address of someone who knows Jeff Buckley's manager. Apparently the manager is having a party right now, and this girl said Jeff might come later. We're going." She cocks her head, addressing Cat and Reid. "You guys could come, if you want to."

I'm not surprised by Nisha's invitation—this is not the first time my ever-magnanimous friend has encouraged strangers to tag along with us. Or the first time that a stranger has been a hot guy who I'm too shy to ask out myself.

"We have to go to dinner at my uncle's apartment." Reid looks at me like this warrants an apology. "I owe him . . . well, a lot. But at the very least showing up for dinner at his apartment."

Before I can consider a response, Cat is shaking her head. Her stack of silver earrings clacks vigorously. "One does not just *pass up* an opportunity to party with *Jeff Buckley*. Let me call my dad and get us out of it." She turns to Nisha. "Where is this thing?"

"520 East Fifth."

Cat claps her hands together once. "I'll use the pay phone on Sixth. We're good to go. *Allons-y.*"

Already Cat and Nisha are halfway out the door. Reid

is frozen in place on his stool, and I watch his face closely, attempting to read whatever he's thinking.

He smiles, then stands. He's taller than I would have thought. Towering. "I'll come for thirty minutes, then I'll head uptown."

"Sure," I say, like we both already know this bit. Like it's a regular game we play.

His eyes soften when he looks down at me; it's as if I've elicited that response in him a thousand times before, and now I am simply remembering it.

Then I feel a falling sensation in my stomach. A plummet.

That is new.

"Lili," he says, and I can't even remember whatever Jeff Buckley just did with his magic hands and his enchanted tongue—my name in Reid's mouth is the most beautiful thing I have ever heard. I would do anything to make him say it again.

"Reid," I respond.

That downturned smile. "Let's see what's happening on Fifth Street."

II

The four of us start hoofing it up five flights of stairs at 520 East Fifth Street, one of those dilapidated but cozy former tenement buildings with both steel bars and flower boxes framing its windows. I almost slip on the worn-smooth black-marble steps twice before the first landing. Each time, Reid's arm shoots out to steady me.

"And your major?" he asks, his hand hovering behind my lower back. He'd successfully guessed I was an NYU student.

"English. Mainly to please my mom. She's an antiques dealer—a successful one—but she regrets that she didn't have a proper liberal arts education."

Even from the stairwell of the building, I can hear the rangy beat of music playing. By the second floor, I can make out the song: "Tugboat" by Galaxie 500. I thought no one else knew about that band.

"But I'm minoring in fine art photography, for myself," I say. Even though he's behind me, I can sense his bottled-up energy, feel that he's reining in his pace to match mine. I let myself say the whole truth. "But also to please my father. He's an art appraiser for an insurance company. By day. But he's also an avid collector. You know Jerry Saltz of *The Village Voice*? He once called my dad's eye 'Nostradamusian.'"

I catch a hint of Reid's scent and feel the impression of his upper arm as his hand reaches for the railing. "Seems like you lucked out with your parents," he says. "A good combination of cool and stable."

Inside the apartment, a series of warren-like rooms is choked with people our age clutching Yuenglings and cigarettes. Sweat and smoke throw a dim fog over the place.

We're trailing behind Nisha and Cat as they scan the rooms for the musician. When they keep not finding him, Nisha's disappointment is discernible, even on the back of her head.

"What about your parents?" I ask Reid. "Too much of one thing?"

"My mom was a backup singer for Crosby, Stills, Nash & Young, which should tell you pretty much everything you need to know about her."

"I disagree. I absolutely need to know more about her."

After we've made a tour of the entire apartment—playing it cool is obviously not the goal here—Nisha turns back to me. "It wasn't meant to be." She does a cartoonish shrug-and-pout thing, but I know she feels betrayed by the workings of fate, which earlier had seemed to be on her side.

Cat slings an arm over her shoulder. "It's still early. Drinking will make the time go faster." She starts to steer Nisha toward the galley kitchen, then stops herself, turning to address Reid: "Don't fuck this up." She swings her finger between the two of us, indicating exactly what it is that Reid must not fuck up.

It seems we've picked up a second wingwoman. I feel my face flush, though whether it's in embarrassment or anticipation, I'm not sure.

"Sorry about my cousin," Reid says when they're out of earshot. He gives me an aggrieved look. "She wouldn't understand subtlety if it punched her in the gut."

I laugh. "Nisha is a lot like that too."

Reid nods toward the kitchen, where we can just make out Cat's buzzed red head over the crowd, then Nisha's cackle, flitting through the crunchy bass of "Cannonball," the new Breeders song I keep hearing on K-Rock. "Kindred spirits. I love my cousin, but I know she can be a lot for some people."

"I like her a lot–ness. Nisha's too. She absorbs the attention from the room, and that leaves me free to be kind of anonymous. Which I want to be, sometimes." I tug at the ends of my hair, which fall almost to my waist, loose and sun bleached.

His eyes skim over my bare shoulders. "Why would you want to be anonymous?"

"So that I can exist without the pressure of performance. I've been trying to let go of that, though."

He considers me, his brows pulled together. "I can see why you're a good photographer."

I raise an eyebrow at him. "You've never seen my photography." My voice has a playful edge, but something in me is giddy at the prospect of Reid seeing my work.

"I don't need to see it to know you're good at it." He reaches up to knead the back of his neck. "For what it's worth, I don't think you could be anonymous if you tried."

A man in a leather bomber jacket and a beret accidentally backs into Reid, which sends him colliding into me. My face presses against the buttons of his shirt. On an inhale, I take in his up-close scent: Underneath the pine, there's something quieter, like laundry detergent rolled in a bed of musk.

This, I think, *is what a man smells like.*

Two big, warm hands wrap around my upper shoulders. Reid is righting me again. "Should we go somewhere we can actually hear each other?"

I gesture to the chaos around us. "Do you think that exists?"

"If you want it, I'll find it."

I nod. He takes my hand and coaxes me through the crowd, eventually leading me to a tiny bedroom in the back of the apartment. It's oddly austere: a twin mattress made up in hospital-cornered maroon sheets with a *Reservoir Dogs* poster hung over it. The only other furniture is a complicated-looking boombox that takes up an entire wall. Miraculously, the room is empty.

"Do you want to keep this open?" He puts his hand on the door.

"You can close it," I nod, but he still leaves it ajar.

There's a window over the flaking radiator. I open it, letting in a gentle rush of humid air and summer city sounds—promise, in audio form.

The window leads out to a fire escape. I've lived in New York for my entire life but somehow have never been out onto one. It's always just felt easier to play it safe. Among other dangers (taper candles, the invisible filth on hotel bedspreads), my mother raised me to believe that you must have a death wish to traverse a fire escape voluntarily. Terrible things are always going to happen, so why make it so easy for them to come to you?

Now I can practically hear her yelling at me as I climb out onto the landing, my platform sandals clanging on the metal.

Reid stays inside the room, leaning cautiously against the windowsill.

"Heights aren't my thing." He reaches out a hand toward me, seemingly on impulse. It brushes the ends of my hair, as if to make sure I'm really there, sitting on a sort-of-sturdy surface and not tumbling five stories down onto the sidewalk.

"Didn't you say you're a screenwriter? You're missing out on some good material here."

"*I* didn't call myself a screenwriter. My cousin did."

Clearly, though, he takes this as a challenge. Behind me, I hear a low *fuck* and feel the metal underneath me vibrate with his added weight.

When he sits next to me, he folds his long legs into his chest and loops his arms loosely around them. He takes a deep inhale and closes his eyes, steadying himself.

"Not so bad, right?" I say.

"Not if I can't see that we're fifty feet off the ground."

"If you keep your eyes closed, you'll miss the little community garden down here. Also the people having sex in front of their window."

It's not an unheard-of thing in New York, to see people having sex in full view of the street, but the timing of it adds something surreal and cinematic to the moment. Reid's eyes are closed, but I still motion across the way, to where a woman's bare breasts are on display. Even from here, I can make out the sated glaze in her eye, her wet mouth half open. I feel a slickness between my legs. I've never considered voyeurism a turn-on, but I've also never had Reid beside me, the coiled promise of his body within reach.

He opens one of his eyes to squint at me. "You're fucking with me."

"I'm not the one fucking right now."

He braves a glance across the street, then turns to look at me again.

"Well, you're right about the material." He rasps a hand over his face. In the failing light, I can see a layer of stubble coming in across his jaw.

"Why are you still looking at me," I say, "and not the woman spread-eagled in plain sight thirty feet across from you?"

He laughs. "Because I don't know her."

"You don't know me either."

"It feels . . . weird. To watch them without their permission. I don't know, I think I need to have more of an emotional connection with someone before anything sexual happens with them."

"That's suspiciously noble of you."

"Must be all the classic movies my mom forced me to watch as a kid."

"Reid." I put a hand on his arm. "I'm going to ask you a serious question: Are you being forced to work in finance against your will?"

A lopsided smile. "My uncle didn't need to give me this job. He probably shouldn't have. But he knew I didn't have anything lined up yet and that I'm reasonably capable of following orders. I think my mom pushed him into it. She knows I've always wanted to live in New York, and I just graduated. Also, Jewish guilt is a powerful thing. If I were to walk back a commitment to her brother, my mom would work it into every single one of our conversations until one of us dies."

"I'm well acquainted with the feeling. So you're not from New York?"

"Is anyone really *from* New York?"

"I am." I point skyward, the universal sign of *uptown*. "I grew up on West Eighty-Sixth Street." He makes a *hm* sound, silently taking in this new information about me. "What about you?"

"I'm from LA." I notice him hesitate for a moment. "My contract at the firm ends next Monday. I only have one more week in New York before I head back."

Monday, which also happens to be my first day of classes. It is rapidly promising to be a terrible day.

"So we're both from places that no one is really from," I say while my mind contemplates whether it is possible to miss a person you barely know. It's sort of an insane thought. "Did you consider going to school here? In New York?" I ask.

"Sure, but money was an issue. When I was in middle school, my mom got a job as an administrative aide at an elementary school. You'd be surprised how many transferable skills she picked up from her groupie days."

"I thought you said she was a backup singer?"

"Technically. But that wasn't the extent of her job description."

He laughs, so I do too. I feel a prick of curiosity about who his dad is. Am I shooting the shit with David Crosby's son right now? My own father would actually die of happiness.

"Anyway," Reid is saying, "my uncle helped us out sometimes, but my mom was too proud to let him fully fund my tuition. It was easier for everyone if I went to a state school. And UCSD has a solid screenwriting program, which is pretty hard to find."

"So what are you going to do when you're home? In LA, I mean."

"Hug my mom."

"And then what?"

I notice it again—his hesitation. I'm starting to sense that he's an overthinker like me. According to my parents, this is also part of what makes me an artist: that I possess an excess of empathy but maintain a clinical, observational distance from all that emotion.

I see myself in him, which means I can tell he's holding

back. I am desperate to get closer to his core, to unearth what it is that's causing a crease to form between his brows.

But also—I'm starting to feel protective of him. *You can do it*, I want to say to him, just like I often want to tell myself. *You can say the hard thing.*

He sighs. "I don't really have a plan. This is kind of embarrassing, but at the beginning of the summer, like in my first week of working at the firm, I was making a hundred copies of a case I could barely understand, and what I did understand of it was so crushingly dull that I could actually feel a part of my soul dying. There was no art in it. I hadn't had a creative thought in weeks. I realized I was miserable. I missed writing. I missed who I *was* when I was writing. So I decided to do something sort of risky."

He looks over at me, like he's making sure I'm still with him. In the distance, I hear the twinkle of a glass breaking, a muffled cackle, and something too fast and violent playing on the sound system—Minor Threat or Circle Jerks, one of the older hardcore bands. I can't explain it, but I already know that this will be one of those moments I'll feel nostalgic for in years or decades to come—that this is one of those instants from which the rest of my life will unfurl.

I nod at him, coaxing him along.

On a breath, he says, "I sent the screenplay I'd submitted as my thesis to Jake Bellingham."

I find it ridiculously sweet that he considers mailing a screenplay to a stranger "risky." Especially because I have never heard that name in my life.

When I don't respond, he cocks his head. "He wrote *Forgive Me*?"

I know this one, of course—the movie about the lapsed Catholic priest who descends into a sex addiction. It swept the Oscars a couple years ago.

"He writes scripts that read like novels. His characters are super complex, and it's like every word they say has a second, deeper meaning beneath it. He's the kind of artist who depresses me a little, because I know I'll never be that good, but it's also exciting—he's making the format feel so much more expansive." He runs a hand over his face and sighs. "So, yeah. I sent him the script with a cover letter that was probably way too fawning. I told myself I wasn't expecting an answer, but now it's been over two months, which probably means an answer is never coming. I'm disappointed, and I feel stupid for being disappointed."

"So you really are a rebel."

"And I used the office machine to make a copy."

"You belong in jail."

He laughs. The strap of my dress has fallen halfway down my shoulder, revealing the swath of skin between my breast and my arm that I've always secretly found elegant. That I've always wanted someone else to admire. I feel Reid's eyes drift right to that spot, and then, as he remembers himself, quickly shift back up to meet my face.

I am suddenly aware, unselfconsciously, that I am being perceived by this man in exactly the way that I've yearned to be: unburdened, charismatic, like I, too, might have a second, deeper meaning. I want to tell him that he can keep looking; that I want him to. That, somehow, I feel safer within the cradle of his gaze than outside of it. He doesn't need to leave the door open for me. I don't want anyone else to find me here.

"I'm worried about what time it is." I realize I'm whispering, that suddenly this moment feels so fragile. "But I don't want you to leave the party."

"I don't really want to leave either. But I'm free tomorrow night. And the night after that. And—I don't want to be presumptuous here—but also the night after that."

"But you won't be here next week."

He leans back on his hands, tilting his head to seek out the invisible stars above. "No, I won't be here next week. I'll be back in LA then."

A pit opens up in my stomach. It is absurd, really, how much dread I feel at the prospect of a person I barely know not sitting next to me a few days from now.

But the boundaries of time also create a sense of safety, and I resolve to treat this as a test: How deeply can I allow myself to feel? How much can I release myself, to really transform into the person I think I can become—the one I feel like I am when in his gaze? If I fail, if my shell refuses to crack, if I'm halting and unsure and overthinking, then there will be no repercussions—no potential humiliation, no lingering awkwardness. Reid will simply disappear from my life, securely tucked away on the opposite coast, and I'll never risk seeing him again.

But then, I can't quite acknowledge that those are also the repercussions if I succeed.

Reid turns to look at me again. The little rambling garden below us is spangled in fairy lights, and it's like each tiny bulb has unlatched and floated up here to glitter in his eyes.

You're done for, I think, counting every tiny flash. I don't even want to hide from his prolonged eye contact—that's how much I like this guy.

He slowly raises his hand, and his knuckles graze my cheek. I lean into his touch, desperate for more and prepared to plunge headfirst into the challenge I've laid out for myself.

So I lean in and kiss him. When our lips meet, there's less a spark than a current, like a circuit being completed. His fingers reach for the hair at the nape of my neck that's frizzing with the humidity, and I thrill in that private scent of him, clean and musky at once.

But the sound of my name breaks the spell: It's Nisha, yelling for me from the bedroom. Cat's voice, yelling for Reid, follows.

Panic crosses Reid's features. We get up and climb back into the room.

I see Nisha's face first, glistening with tears. Before I can ask her what's wrong, Cat grabs Reid and me both by the arms.

"He's here," Cat says. Her tone is hushed and reverent. "Jeff Buckley is fucking *here*."

III

"Do you feel like you're in a fever dream?" Reid asks. He neatly folds a piece of lettuce back into his sandwich. "Because I do."

"I absolutely do," I say.

We're in Bryant Park, sitting at one of the green cast-iron tables that look like dollhouse set pieces. The heat from yesterday is holding on, but we've managed to find a slice of shade in the shadow of the library. Today I'm in an outfit that won't show sweat: a navy cotton dress that hits right at my upper thighs, my hair twirled up into a claw clip.

Reid's jacket is off and his sleeves are rolled up, but his tie is still knotted around his neck. He barely seems to notice the heat, though. I realize I've known him for under twenty-four hours, but those twenty-four hours have been some of the hottest on record, and I have yet to witness this man perspire.

I watch the long lines of his body settle back into his comically tiny chair.

Before Reid left the party last night—twenty minutes later than he'd needed to—we exchanged numbers and made plans to have dinner tonight. But he'd called me this morning and asked if I wanted to meet him on his lunch break too.

I don't want to wait until seven to see you, he'd said.

I'd intended to spend the day finally preparing for the upcoming semester and catching up on the required reading I've failed to do—but this invitation made those things feel impossible.

"How's Nisha holding up?" Reid says now.

"We're hoping she'll make a full recovery by 1994."

I'm proud of how Nisha kept her cool last night. After she retrieved us from the bedroom, she dried off her face, touched up her eyeliner, and headed back out into the party. We found Jeff Buckley sitting on the floor of the living room, leaning against the couch and thoughtfully nursing a beer, surrounded by wide-eyed acolytes. The scene brought to mind a sixteenth-century painting my mother discovered in a dusty garage in Jakarta, one depicting a young, svelte Buddha lounging underneath a banyan tree, encircled by his lotus-posed followers. The Buddha was rendered in gold leaf so pure that, according to the dealer who sold it to her, centuries of aspiring art thieves had attempted to scrape the pigment off and sell it. None succeeded, due either to some ingenious preservative mixed into the paint or good old-fashioned karma, depending on the eye of the beholder.

In the few minutes we spent observing Jeff on the floor of that party, he didn't speak once, though all conversation was subtly directed toward him. His eyes alighted on me—he saw everyone, I think—but they seemed to look right through me, like he had access to another higher vibrational plane of existence. I didn't particularly like the way it felt.

When Nisha worked up the courage to crawl over and tell him she was a fan, he finally spoke. I couldn't hear a single word they exchanged, so my transcript comes directly from Nisha, who recounted it to me at least three times on the walk home, and then again this morning, when she burrowed into my bed and, with the clarity of retrospect and soberness, burst into tears of overwhelm.

Nisha: I'm a huge fan of yours.

Jeff: That's lovely to hear. I appreciate it.

End scene.

"It's nice that the whole 'don't meet your heroes' thing doesn't apply to Nisha's experience. That she doesn't regret it," Reid says now.

"Have you ever done that?" I ask. "Met your heroes, I mean."

He considers this for a moment. "Maybe not a personal hero, but my mom stayed friends with a few of the musicians she knew from Laurel Canyon, even after we moved out to Altadena. Some of them were really famous. One time, I think when I was four or five, Stephen Stills came out there to spend the day with us. He picked lemons from the tree in our neighbor's yard and made us lemonade."

"How was that?"

"He put, like, half a pound of sugar in it, so I had a great time."

I laugh. He gestures to the plastic cup I grabbed from the deli along with the sandwiches I'd picked up for our lunch.

"How's that?" He peers into my drink.

"Want to try?"

He leans across the table just enough to grab the straw with his teeth while I hold the cup for him. I watch the strong lines of his throat work while he swallows, his eyes trained on mine.

This, I think, *is the most intimate thing I've done with anyone in a long time. Maybe ever.*

He sits back down. "Better than Stephen's."

"Thanks. Tropicana is responsible for the recipe. But I did dispense it into this cup myself."

"You've got a bright future ahead of you."

"How lucrative a field is drink-dispensing, do you think?" It's a dumb joke, but he laughs anyway. I've never made a guy laugh this easily, and it feels *so right*, like the click of a shutter that captures a singular, impossible moment. I sigh. "Well, good, because I can feel my job prospects diminishing with every passing minute."

"Why's that?" His face goes serious.

"School is . . . tough for me right now. I haven't done a single thing to prepare for this semester. I keep putting it off, saying I'll do it tomorrow. I don't even remember what classes I signed up for."

I wasn't planning on dragging school into this conversation. I don't want him to think that I'm a slacker, or that I'm not grateful to go to NYU. But there's something about the way Reid is looking at me that makes me want to open up, to share this small, seemingly manageable thing that's somehow become gargantuan and swallowed me in anxiety.

"What do you have to do to prepare?" There's no trace of judgment in his words. Just a matter-of-fact question to gather information and see what we can do with it. It instantly makes me feel calmer.

"I need to look over all my syllabi and then buy books. That's probably the most pressing thing."

"Why don't we do that tonight? I can meet you at the NYU bookstore after work. Or wherever you get your books."

"Really? You would do that with me?"

"Yeah, of course. When I was in middle school, I went through a pretty serious procrastination phase, and the only thing that got me through it was when my mom would sit down at the kitchen table with me while I did my homework. She didn't even help, unless I asked for it. Just her presence, her sitting there with me, was enough."

I must be looking at him for too long, or with too much sincerity, because at some point, he asks if I'm OK.

"Yeah," I say. "That's just, like, the nicest thing anyone has ever offered to do for me."

A furrow forms between his brows. He leans in toward me, so close I can see that his eyes are not really brown but terracotta, shot through with pale gold flecks.

"I don't like that." He says it earnestly. I can feel his warm breath drape across my mouth. *Closer*, I think. *More.* "I want people to be nice to you."

I'm touched by this show of simple, righteous indignation. Is he starting to feel protective of me?

I don't respond, too overwhelmed. I think Reid senses this. He stands, sweeps all our wrappers into the paper deli bag, then reaches out his hand for mine.

I walk him the three blocks back to his office. He keeps hold of my hand as we navigate around the crush of suits and tourists milling around Midtown. I leave him at the bottom of the stairs that lead up to his building—it's imposing, faceless, and it makes me sad to think of him buried in there, another cog in a machine that's too big for me to understand—but he nobly puts his jacket back on, straightens the lapels, and rearranges the cuffs of his shirt.

Before I leave, he kisses me on the forehead. "See you tonight."

"Grisham, Steele, Crichton."

"Steele," I say without pause.

"Wow. Not even a little bit of hesitation."

"If I can only read one author for the rest of my life, they need to have a healthy catalog. She'll keep me entertained. OK, here's one for you: Stephen King, Jay McInerney, Thomas Hardy."

"Doesn't Jay McInerney only have, like, two books? I'm going with Stephen King."

I shiver. "I'd go with Thomas Hardy. I can't do horror."

Reid and I are deep in the stacks at the NYU bookstore.

After lunch, I went home, opened up the envelopes that had been inflicting so much misery upon me for the last week, and discovered that, actually, now that I've faced it, I could sort of look forward to my first day of classes: Brit Lit at noon and a portraiture workshop at three. My sophomore-year self had looked out for my junior-year self, keeping my mornings open until eleven at the earliest and my Fridays free, other than a Psych 101 lecture at one that I could skip a couple of times if I wanted to, or at least bury myself in the back of the cavernous lecture hall unnoticed by the professor.

When we got to the bookstore, Reid and I collected all the titles I needed surprisingly quickly. *Works well with others*, I thought, watching him scan my list and navigate between each section of the store. Never in my life have I found efficiency so sexy. We've rewarded ourselves with a trip to the quiet basement.

It's near closing time now, and only two or three other people are down here, loitering around the memoir section, too engrossed in their own browsing to notice us.

Reid is walking ahead of me, but now he turns, gives me one of those upside-down smiles that I've started to collect like currency. "Really? No horror?"

I rebalance the pile of books under my arms. Wordlessly, he holds his hands out and does a little beckoning motion with his fingers. I give him the pile, which he carries easily against his side.

"Yeah." I follow him farther into the stacks. "When I was ten, I caught a few minutes of *Psycho* on TV, and it scared the shit out of me. After that, I had to shower with the curtain partially open. I really wanted my mom to sit with me in the bathroom, but she'd never coddle me like that."

"You still showering with the curtain open?"

I laugh. "No."

"Ah. Too bad."

And now I'm imagining Reid leaning against my bathroom sink, fully clothed, watching me naked with water streaming over my body. The look in his eyes is satisfied, smug. He reaches out to run his knuckles across my nipple, then across my hip, lower to my thigh . . .

Reid—the real Reid—interrupts my fantasy. "OK, so we won't be watching *Misery* together. How do you feel about supernatural stuff?"

He pulls the corner of a book off a high shelf, considers it, then slots it back into place. I have no idea which section of the store we're even in now. I'm too focused on the way his shoulder blades shift underneath his white shirt when he reaches for a book, how his scent flares and intensifies in this enclosed space.

"I'm OK with supernatural stuff. I'm not scared of monsters; I'm scared of humans."

"So maybe there's a chance you'll like my screenplay." He says this to the shelf, like he's too shy to address me directly.

"You wrote a fantasy script?"

He laughs. "You seem surprised."

"I just didn't know you were that kind of nerd."

"I am one hundred percent that kind of nerd. But

this isn't, like, *Lord of the Rings* high fantasy. My brain doesn't work that way, unfortunately. I'm thinking of it as a dramedy with fantastical elements." He glances at me and I smile, waiting for the elevator pitch. "A guy moves in with his girlfriend and discovers that her roommates are vampires and she's their human familiar. But he can't tell her he knows."

"Secret vampires!"

"Think *The Lost Boys* meets *Moonstruck* meets *Slacker*."

"I honestly don't know what that means, but I would love to read it, if you want me to."

"Of course I want you to."

We're at the farthest end of the stacks now, crowded against the wall. He turns to face me. Slowly, he puts my books down on the floor, freeing himself up for me. With one more step, I wrap my arms around his waist and press my nose against his shirt, and he encircles my shoulders in his lean, strong arms. All those movements happen at the same time, a bow tying itself.

We hold each other like that for a moment, and then I tilt my head back to look up into his face.

"If you read my screenplay, can I see some of your photographs?" he asks.

"What do you want to see?"

"Anything you make, I want to see."

"OK. Deal."

His hand reaches up to cup my face, the tips of his fingers tangling in the hair at the nape of my neck again. He rubs his thumb against my bottom lip. Once, I read in *Cosmo* that if a man keeps looking at your mouth, it means he wants to kiss you. What does it mean, then, if he presses the pad of his thumb between your lips? What does it mean when you close your lips around his thumb and take it into your mouth? When you look up into his face and the glassy look in his eyes makes everything inside you coil tightly, begging to be teased and released?

He pulls his thumb out of my mouth with a wet *pop*. The sound is audible and filthy inside the quiet room.

His eyes scan between mine, seeking something—something more. Of me.

When he speaks, his voice is low. "Should we go to dinner?"

I forgot we'd planned to eat at Cafe Mogador—an East Village institution that Reid absolutely needs to go to before he leaves—and that, up until three minutes ago, I was really looking forward to introducing him to the stunning beauty of their hot, crispy falafel.

But that was before I knew what his skin tastes like. Before I knew how he looks at me when I have him in my mouth.

"Let's not go to dinner," I say.

His hands drop to my chin, my neck, my shoulders. I know he's taking his time with me, making sure I feel secure, but if he doesn't kiss me right now, I think that I will die.

Finally, I get his lips when they graze behind my ear—soft and full, with the barest press of teeth.

I feel his breath skate down my neck. "Deal," he says.

IV

My apartment is only a fifteen-minute walk from the bookstore, but each block feels agonizingly long. I'm hyperaware of the way Reid's body navigates space, the relative distance between his and mine. With each passing crosswalk, I find myself inching closer to him; when we reach First Avenue, his fingers entwine with mine.

By the time we make it up the three flights to my place, my skin feels like it's on fire, like the stroke of his thumb against the back of my hand might launch me into space.

Nisha is out, so I lead him directly into my bedroom and shut the door all the way. The backs of my legs press against my bed, and I wait for Reid to finally use the weight of his body against mine. But he doesn't. Instead, he just leans against the door, hands behind his back. His eyes rake over me. I wonder what he sees there—the quickening rise and fall of my chest, a wild glint in my expression? The corner of his mouth twists into a smile. It's the cockiest he's ever looked. Heat pools and aches between my legs.

"Come here," I say, quietly.

He runs a hand down his face, letting it come to rest on his chin. "No." The grit in his voice is the only indication that his control might not be as tethered as it seems. "You come to me."

I cross my arms, unsure of how to navigate this demand. "Why?"

"Because if I lay you down on that bed," he says, each word deliberate, "I'm going to fuck you."

My throat catches on a sound halfway between laughter and disbelief. "Reid," I say, carefully. "That's exactly what I want you to do."

He clasps his hands behind his back again, and he shakes his head, like I'm not getting something. "If that happens right now, I'm . . . I want to take my time and enjoy this." He blows out a breath. "Just come here. Please."

When I step in front of him, he immediately drops to his knees, and his hands brace gently behind my legs. I want to ask him what he's doing—no one has ever handled me this way—but I close my eyes and trust him instead. Trust the way my body responds to his movements, how my hands lift to his hair, running through the thick strands, tugging at them gently. *He likes that*, I think, judging from the satisfied sound that escapes from his throat. He slides the straps of my dress down my shoulders, one at a time, then wriggles the dress down over my hips and onto the floor.

He sits back on his heels for a moment, looking up at me, then takes my breasts in his hands and rubs the pads of his thumbs over my nipples, sliding the flat of his tongue over each one, coaxing them to tight nubs. A sound comes out of me that I'm not sure I've ever heard before, choked and desperate, and he offers a deep, pleasured groan in return. The reverberation of it vibrates against my skin. I think that I might come like that, with his head against my chest, the feel of his tongue stroking my skin. The pride he takes in my pleasure.

His hands move to my hips, his fingertips toying with the seam of my underwear, then hooking along the sides. He fists the fabric in his hands.

Reid looks up at me again. "Can I touch you now?" he asks, his voice threatening to break.

I nod. "Please take them off."

Instead, he turns me so I'm leaning my back against the door, then pushes my underwear to the side.

"Wider." He breathes the words against my skin. He wraps a hand around the back of each of my thighs.

I don't have time to think about being so exposed, being positioned in a way that makes us both so vulnerable. The force of my desire quiets my inner monologue, and when Reid licks me once—insistent, searching—thoughts evaporate entirely. I give myself over to his eager mouth, his probing fingers. His need for me unlocks an entirely new dimension of my need for him.

When his thumb begins to rub circles against my clit, I orgasm, my entire body trembling above him, boneless and liquid, but Reid maintains his hold on my hips to keep me upright. I tug at his hair again, already anticipating the hitch of his breath.

"I've never come from that before," I admit once I regain control over coherent thought.

In the past, I've always been too self-conscious to let go entirely, and much too shy to say what I want. And that's on the rare occasion I've been with someone who dared to go down on me at all.

Reid drops his head, almost bashful. When he looks back up at me, a small smile plays at his lips. He looks gratified, wrung out. Still a little cocky.

"If I told you how good that makes me feel, would that make me an asshole?"

I laugh. "Definitely not."

"Good," he says. Then he stands to his full height, presses his body against me, and leans down to melt me into a deep, slow kiss. I feel the weight of his cock against my bare thigh, and I wriggle against him to lodge him between my legs. He lets out a long, pained groan.

"OK," he says in my ear, exhaling a laugh. "This is when you get on the bed."

Reid needs to leave my apartment the next morning at an ungodly hour so he can head back to his uncle's apartment, shower, change, and get to the office by eight. Before we'd fallen asleep, he'd set my alarm clock to 4:30 a.m. But when it springs to screeching life, I'm already awake, and have been the entire night.

How could I sleep with Reid in my bed—his arms around me, his skin against my skin, his breath against my ear? I'd stayed awake, constructing futures from the raw material of his proximity. We would split pastries on slow weekend mornings, lick the cream and the sugar off each other's fingers. He would pick me up from class, his tie undone, his suit jacket flung over one shoulder, and I would witness, in real time, the way his thoughtful expression breaks open with joy when he sees me. I imagine all the blissful mundanities of partnered life that I've never experienced before—had observed in other people, in books and songs and smitten passersby. Had simply considered as an abstract, faraway thing that maybe, one day, could be nice to have for myself.

I know that I'm anticipating scenarios that will probably never exist. But I can't stop myself from thinking of them. It just feels too good to stop.

Reid rolls over to face me. In his semiconscious state, his expression is unguarded, soft. For a moment, I wonder whether he'll be happy to find himself here, waking up next to me. Or whether he'll retract and bolt, like most twentysomething guys.

"Hi," he says. He folds the sheet down over me, uncovering my naked body, then takes my breast in his hand—an instinctive, almost possessive action, at odds with the sweetness of his smile, the gentleness of his tone.

I move closer toward him. "Can I make you breakfast?" The question surprises me as I ask it—I've never cooked anything more complicated than noodles with jarred marinara sauce. But the urge to nourish him feels elemental.

He laughs, a mixture of surprise and shyness. "I think this is an offer I can't refuse."

"Do you doubt my breakfast-making skills?"

"Not at all." He pauses, calibrating for honesty. "I've just never had a girl make me breakfast before. It's strange." When he sees the way I retreat, suddenly embarrassed, he gently tugs at my wrist, prompting me to face him again. "Not strange in a bad way. Strange how normal it feels for you to be the one to ask me that question."

Normal. I'd never thought the concept of normalcy could make me wet. And when my hand drifts down his chest, down to his cock, I find him hard.

Reid's hands bracket my waist, pulling me on top of him so our torsos align. His eyes go soft when I open my thighs around him, and his hands grip me tighter when I begin to rock against him.

The sex we had last night had been rushed and feverish, clumsy in our desperation to get inside each other's skin. There's no less urgency now, but there is a delicious laziness in Reid's movements, in the satisfied way his teeth press into his lower lip when I release a moan. He's taking his time with me.

Trying to, anyway.

I lift my hips high enough for Reid to graze a finger between my legs. A whispered *fuck* when he feels how slick I am. My hips buck against him, not quite full enough.

Reading my movements, he presses his mouth against my jaw. "You want more?"

I nod, my exhale breaking into a moan when he slips himself inside me and he finally, finally, fills me up entirely. I want him to move so badly, but he just holds himself in place, like maybe that will stop time from spinning away from us.

In the pause, I wonder, again, what the hell we are doing here. How I have made this person materialize in my life, and how quickly I know he is going to dissolve.

I can't take the stillness anymore. I glide against him once, enough to snap his control and start fucking me for real, steady and insistent.

I let myself believe in this. I let myself go.

Eventually, we go to the bodega down the block and pick up a carton of eggs, a sleeve of white bread, and to-go coffees in Greek-key cups. He laughs when I dump two pods of cream and three sugars into mine.

"That's not coffee," he says. "That's a milkshake."

I point to the steaming black liquid he lifts to his mouth. "That's not coffee. That's motor oil."

At home, I take a stab at making over-easy eggs on the only burner that works. When I bring his plate to the table, Reid pulls gently at my hair, tugging me down for a kiss.

I love watching the way he arranges each forkful, neatly stacking each bite onto the tip and sliding it down the tines. At one point, he stops, drops his silverware, and gives me an amused look.

"What is it?"

With my chin, I gesture toward his plate. "Enjoying yourself?"

“I am. Are you enjoying critiquing my neuroses?”

“I’m not critiquing. I’m admiring.”

The look he gives me—devilish, conspiratorial—makes my thighs clench. He picks up his fork and knife and slices his last over-easy egg into four evenly sized pieces. One by one, he puts them in his mouth, chews, and swallows. He maintains eye contact with me throughout this performance. I feel my face flush, my heart kick into double-time.

“Were you aware,” he says, dabbing his mouth with a napkin, “that you had a neat-eating kink?”

I take a sip of water. “I don’t think I have a neat-eating kink,” I say. “I think I have a Reid kink.”

I brace myself for his response. Lili before Reid never would have said such a thing.

But he sits back into his chair, crosses his arms, and gives me an appraising look.

“That works out nicely,” he says. “Because I think I have a Lili kink.”

V

On Thursday, Cat gets a hold of her dad's platinum card and takes Reid, Nisha, and me out for cocktails at Bemelmans Bar, the storied lounge inside The Carlyle Hotel. Reid doesn't even ask what underhanded methods she used to secure it, and I take his lack of concern as an indicator of how soon he's really leaving. His time here is too precious to play the role of moral compass, to keep us away from a good time.

In his work suit and with his impeccable manners, Reid is the only one of us who looks marginally at home in this hushed, elegantly perfumed room. I barely had time to change when Cat called with the news that she'd absconded with the card and to meet her uptown in twenty minutes, before her father discovered his wallet a few grams lighter. I threw on a black jersey boatneck minidress—one of the nicer things I own—but I didn't have a chance to brush my hair. On the sidewalk outside, Reid had attempted to unravel the tiny knots from the fine wisps at my nape.

The maître d' stashes us in a booth in the back corner. We all order martinis. Reid stops Cat from adding Ossetra caviar.

We carefully clink the edges of our glasses together, trying so hard not to lose any of our ten-dollar cocktails to the table. Still, the toast sends a glug of Cat's drink over the edge of her glass.

"To this summer," Cat declares. "Thanks for the opportunity to smoke pure Sour D on various river-view rooftops. You've been good to me."

"To the Urban Homesteading Assistance Board," Nisha says. "May they one day grant us the ability to run electric legally."

After her Jeff Buckley moment at the party, Nisha met a trombonist named Pepper, who lives in C-Squat. Over the past few days, she's been spending most of her time over there, helping the tenants repair the broken staircase and prep the radiators ahead of winter. She's energized by communal living, says she's found purpose in contributing her time and energy to a greater cause. She recruited me to volunteer my own skills too, which in my case means documenting the scene with my camera.

Yesterday I captured one of the tenants, a hardcore guy with a tattooed skull and pet rat perched on his shoulder, delicately tending to a row of lemon balm growing in the community garden.

"Brew this shit up, add some local honey, and it'll cure all your ills," he told me after giving me permission to take his photograph. Then he snipped off a fistful of leaves and stuffed them in my hand. *Does imminent heartbreak count?* I'd wanted to ask him, but stopped myself from being so dramatic.

As much as I love Nisha's passion, I also worry, selfishly, that she will abandon me for her newfound community—she'll move out of our apartment, spend her time on nobler causes and with people with so much more purpose than me. I worry that I'll be left behind.

Time rushes through my hands, impervious to my feelings about it. But I am desperate for more of it—with my friends, next to Reid, at this beautiful bar with its tinkling piano and a very full glass.

"To Christian Slater hosting the VMAs," I say, refusing to let myself go maudlin. "Surely the most boring choice of a host in awards show history. May he prove us all wrong with his wit and charm."

This is not the time for melancholy. This drink is too expensive to cry into.

"Whatever the MTV execs are snorting is really not working for them," Nisha agrees.

"To the New Yorkers at the table," Reid says. He looks at each of us for a beat, and then his gaze lingers on mine. "Thank you for making me feel at home here."

Cat pats Reid's cheek with the back of her hand. "Good boy," she says. Reid swats her away.

"This is cute as hell for us." Nisha takes a loud slurp. "Let's do it again next week."

We keep going like that—shooting the shit, making jokes, ribbing each other. But I latch on to what Nisha just said, surely by accident. My attention keeps drifting forward. Reid pulls my hand into his lap. I know what he's doing: He's comforting me. We don't talk about next week. Next week he'll be gone.

The next morning, Reid gets ready to leave my apartment at the usual predawn hour to head back uptown for work. He may be on his way out of this job, he tells me, and he might hate it with every fiber of his being, but he refuses to start looking sloppy now. It would reflect badly on his uncle. He can't show him that kind of disrespect.

I catch his hand before he climbs out of bed. The sun is just beginning to reveal itself through my flimsy white curtains, and the light catches Reid's form in a brilliant outline.

"Why don't you just stay here this weekend?" I say. "Nisha's planning to sleep at the Squat until they finish the radiator installation."

"You wouldn't mind a six-foot dude in your five-hundred-square-foot apartment?"

I love his voice. Deep, self-assured, but still with a boyish, Southern California lilt to it. His lips, his teeth. I want to take them all in my mouth, to consume the mint and the velvet and the sunshine. The sound of him alone is enough to send a pulse thrumming between my legs.

"Not if the six-foot dude smells as good as you do."

He grins at me. "OK, yeah. I'll bring some stuff over after work."

He plants a kiss on my forehead, then turns to head to the bathroom. But the sensation of unfinished business nags at me. There is something I haven't asked him yet, and I can't focus on anything else until I do.

I think back to the vow I made to myself on the fire escape: Start being braver than you feel. At least *pretend*. Reid has made this experiment easier, but he's leaving so soon, and I worry that without the shine of him, all that courage will wilt.

I prop myself up on my elbows. "If circumstances were different, do you think you would want to stay in New York?"

This is not the most direct way to say what I mean—*Do you want to be my boyfriend? Do you want to try this for real?*—but he reads between the lines. Reid comes back into the bedroom, shirtless and clenching my toothbrush in his mouth. Then he removes it and assumes a theatrically contemplative pose: resting one knee on the bed, crossing his arms over his bare chest. He looks pensively out the window.

"I've thought about this a lot. How easily or not easily certain circumstances can be changed. There are the logistical ones, like finding a place to live and getting a job, which are daunting, but doable. But I also worry about leaving my mom alone on the West Coast. I know this sounds ridiculous, but it's just been me and her ever since my dad left when I was a baby. I know she's capable of doing things on her own. But I also think she needs me more than she would ever admit."

Then he looks at me directly. His candor ends the game. I feel my face heat beneath his gaze.

"I would do it, though. Despite all that, I would take the risk."

What I hear: *Yes, I would want to be your boyfriend. I would take the risk for you.*

Suddenly, he turns to rifle through his bag, then comes back to the bed with a slim white envelope. It's addressed to him at his work address in blocky, all-caps handwriting.

He hands me the piece of mail, silently offering me permission to open it. I don't know why, but my hands are shaking as I pull out a sheet of folded-up paper, ripped neatly from a yellow legal pad.

I realize, suddenly, that I barely know Reid at all. What secrets has he hidden from me? What terrible truth might he reveal to me now, when he knows he can escape in a few days?

I unfold the paper and scan it, picking up on a handful of words: Brilliant. Promising. Shades of. Would you. New work.

All at once, I understand what I'm looking at: It's a letter from Jake Bellingham, the screenwriter Reid reached out to earlier this summer and from whom he never expected to receive an answer. His personal hero. I read the letter more closely. Bellingham likes his script, sees promise in his work, and is now inviting Reid to come on as a research assistant for a new Miramax project he's leading. The rate is negotiable. He'd need to start on Monday, August 30. That's just over a week from today.

I don't say anything as I try to recenter myself. I'm overwhelmed with pride, and that alone is so alarming. I think back to Nisha explaining the concept of *compersion* to me: feeling authentic joy for another person's joy.

But I'm also crushed. I see our potential future fade from view. I'm envious of Jake Bellingham, and Reid's mother, and—*don't think it, don't say it*—whatever girl he's surely going to fall in love with as soon as his plane touches down at LAX. All the people who get to have him instead of me.

When I look up, I find Reid searching for me, a mixture of pride and anticipation in his expression.

"It came in the mail yesterday," he explains. He's speaking in gentle, measured tones, the way someone might talk to a wild horse. Just this once, I wish he wouldn't be so nice to me. It would make everything so much easier. "I don't know why I didn't tell you about it sooner. I guess I just knew it would make it all real if I did."

"It's amazing," I say, and I really, truly mean it. "It's your dream, right?"

He huffs out a laugh. "Yeah. I guess it is."

"You deserve it. Your script is so interesting and smart. I've never read anything like it before. I'm glad he saw that too."

"So you think I should do it?"

"How could you not do it?"

He flops onto the bed against the pillows, then runs his hands over his face. "Yeah. How could I not."

I can hear the hesitation in his tone, and I am in an

impossible position: I know that he would stay here, and try this, if only I would tell him not to take the job. I wish that I could do that.

But I can't. I may have hardly any experience with relationships, but I'm smart enough to know that depriving someone of their dream is not a good start.

And what if staying in New York didn't work out? What if he struggled to find a job? Or, what if he did find a job, but it was another one that sapped his joy? What if he didn't end up actually liking New York? What if the noise and the pace grated on him? Our sunsets don't even come close to California's. Our winters are a horror show. Two weeks ago, a man tried to pee on me in the subway.

And what if he started to dream of the life he could have lived in LA, and he became resentful that I encouraged him to make the wrong decision, and his resentment turned us bitter, then tore us apart, then left him with nothing, stranded on the other side of the country, so far away from home?

No. I can't.

My eyes are unblinking, and that's when I know it: I'm falling in love with him. Not keeping him here will inflict a kind of emotional violence on me, but I'd rather take on that pain than hold him back from what is very clearly a once-in-a-lifetime opportunity.

I run my hand along his arm, bringing its soothing weight down across my stomach. "You're going to be famous," I say.

He laughs. "I would be the worst famous person." Then

he's quiet, contemplative for a beat. "All my paparazzi shots would just be me going to my mom's house and Ralphs."

"But you'd be looking so cool and aloof while you're doing it."

We lay there in mutual silence, the wooden floorboards catching the first spears of light, collecting in pools around my stacks of paperbacks, the piles of clothes we discarded so urgently last night. We don't need to say anything else. The decision has been made, and we both know that it's a terrible one. But it's the right one too.

I tell myself that I don't need to start saying goodbye to him now. That it's not the end yet.

But time is a bandit, a slippery motherfucker. Over the next three days, we try to pin it down and magnify it. We sip wine from juice glasses on my fire escape, which we're no longer afraid to enjoy. We sun ourselves on the stoop of the Ukrainian church on Seventh Street. We play rainy-afternoon pool at Doc Holliday's against a pair of friendly Hell's Angels. We see a punk show at C-Squat, led by Pepper on his squealing trombone. We squeeze ourselves into a listening booth at Generation Records, sharing a pair of headphones and making out.

There are meals we make in the single pot I own: spaghetti with breadcrumbs, white chicken chili, cold borscht that stains our fingers electric pink. There is stumbling out of Pyramid Club just as a pair of early morning joggers swish by in their neon-yellow shorts. There is a trip to the gem hall at the Natural History Museum, which feels like the inside of a black velvet jewel box. We kiss in the shadow of a gigantic amethyst slice.

There is the feeling of my heart splitting apart when I watch him scrub my pot with a checkered towel thrown over his shoulder. There is the reading I avoid so I can look at him instead. There is the plane ticket he's using as a bookmark that I pretend not to notice.

There's riding the F all the way down to Coney Island, where we take in a sword-swallowing sideshow and watch the hot orange sun flicker beneath the horizon on the boardwalk. Reid looks at home here, with the water and the sunset, so close to the sand. A California boy after all. I have my proof.

I wish I had met you earlier, I want to say. *I wish we hadn't wasted so much of our summer not knowing each other. I wish I could have liberated you from that crushing Midtown high-rise, that I could've shown you the fucked-up beauty of this city from the start, the way it spits its life at you. That you would've fallen in love so hard that you had no choice but to stay.*

There is a marathon walk uptown, ducking into the luxury department stores for the bracing refuge of their air-conditioned lobbies. There is regret that I wore my stupid jelly sandals that make my feet sweat and squeak and rub blisters into my heels, a pain that's at least familiar.

There is waiting outside his uncle's building while he packs the rest of his stuff. There is worry. There is berating myself for not being selfish enough to make him stay, then berating myself some more for such a stupid line of thought. There is chipping my green nail polish with my teeth. There is Cat, emerging from the marble building like a Cherry Cola fairy, embracing me in a musky hug, and telling me that this is not a death, even though it kind of feels like it is.

There is splurging on a cab back downtown, Reid's suitcase stuffed into the trunk like a shameful secret. There is the two of us, not leaving my apartment for the rest of the day so that we can sleep and talk and fuck and not think about a single thing.

And then there is Monday. And then he is gone.

PART II

2023

VI

As the band plays, the screen behind the stage loops video footage of Sin-é in the nineties. Jeff Buckley in his white T-shirt and combat boots, sending the audience into bouts of barely contained ecstasy. A table of young women, commiserating over coffee and cigarettes. A flash of Sinéad O'Connor, elegant and ferocious, performing underneath the Sin-é banner. The footage is grainy and sepia-toned, captured with shaky camcorders. It all looks old-fashioned to me.

I laugh at myself. *What does that make me, then?*

The frontwoman, a twentysomething with waist-length braids and a voice like suede, swaps her acoustic guitar for an electric one and strums the first crunchy, sexy chords of "Yard of Blonde Girls." The guitar is a white Telecaster. The sight of it alone floods me with longing.

It's the same guitar Jeff Buckley played at the Sin-é show in 1993. The show that I still think of as *our* show.

Emme taps my elbow. "You OK, Mom?"

I look up at my daughter—she inherited her father's height, to his unending satisfaction—and I notice the crease in her smooth, perpetually dewy brow. She's been wearing her blond hair in a pair of pink-dipped space buns these days. For the concert tonight, she braided it before swirling it into the buns, then lined her eyebrows in stick-on rhinestones. She's wearing an Edwardian lace nightgown and a pair of cherry-red cowboy boots, both thrifted.

"It's giving Gwen Stefani circa *Return of Saturn*," I told Emme, when she emerged from her vanilla-scented bedroom earlier tonight.

She shot me a lovingly stern look. "Mom," she said, with long-suffering patience. "Please never say *it's giving*."

At fifteen, she's somehow approaching the age I was then. The passage of time was never so punishingly obvious until I became a parent. I want so badly to encase this moment in amber, to keep my daughter exactly where she is now—at home, with me. Especially since the divorce, I've organized my life into two boxes: Emme and my work. I can't even begin to think about how it will feel when Emme goes to college and that box becomes significantly emptier.

"I'm OK, sweetie," I tell Emme now.

Then I realize I haven't picked up my camera during the past ten minutes of this band's set. They're covering the first three tracks of *Sketches for My Sweetheart the Drunk*, my favorite—but an often overlooked—Jeff Buckley album.

"You fine here for a bit?" I ask.

"I've been coming to Webster Hall since I was six." Emme rolls her eyes, and the rhinestones above them sparkle. "I'm gonna go to the bathroom anyway."

I make my way up to the lip of the stage, flashing my

press badge to the few people who stoically refuse to budge. Overall, this crowd is generous, flexible, joyful. Not the case at every show. But this is hardly every show.

A week ago, Nisha sent me an Instagram post announcing the event: a one-night-only tribute show to Jeff Buckley, honoring the twenty-sixth anniversary of his death in 1997. The owner and two previous employees of the now-defunct Sin-é had hoped to commemorate the twenty-fifth, but COVID prevented that from happening. And the past three years have felt like a single, sprawling, unidentifiable mass anyway. What's the difference between twenty-five and twenty-six?

The hosts had originally planned to put on the event at the club's original venue on St. Mark's Place, but they weren't expecting the thousands of messages from supporters, mourners, and celebrants asking if there was still space for more. Or the number of musicians who reached out asking if there was room for them to contribute a cover.

Can you believe it's been over twenty-five years since he's been gone? Nisha had texted.

Of course, the answer is no. That is always the answer when faced with the relentless march of time.

I remember distinctly where I was when I learned that Jeff Buckley had died: James and I were on our third date at Aquagrill when I got an urgent message on my beeper. It was Nisha: *Call me.* For all my complaints about James, he was nothing but compassionate in that moment, displaying the appropriate amount of concern and understanding when I excused myself from the table, hustled up to the hostess booth, and asked to use their phone.

"He's dead," Nisha said, her voice thick with fresh tears. My mind went blank, then kaleidoscopic with a riotous montage of every important man in our lives to whom she might be referring. Bill Clinton? Her father? *My* father?

"Jeff Buckley is dead."

My knees buckled in relief, and then in potent despair. If someone as alive and electric as him could leave this earth so violently, what hope was there for the rest of us?

I couldn't help bringing up Nisha's call when I texted her back: *It feels like just yesterday that you ruined my date with James.*

Nisha responded instantly, despite the fact that it was 4 a.m. in Seattle, where she's been living for the past few months to help care for her father.

Nisha: Didn't stop you from marrying the guy.
Me: Clearly I should've taken Jeff's death as an omen.
Nisha: No comment.
Me: None needed.
Nisha: You have to go to this show for us.
Nisha: And take Emme. Show her how cool we used to be.

But I didn't want to just go. I wanted to be part of it, to somehow mark what it meant to me. And though I've been lucky to make a living as an artist through commercial work, I've always harbored a soft spot for concert photography, though the format rarely suits my schedule or income needs as a single parent. So few public experiences are as transcendent as live music. No matter how intimate I am with a portrait subject, I can never get them to release themselves as fully as their favorite musician can.

So I reached out to one of the co-organizers and offered my services for free. I only told my agent, Hayes, when the gig was confirmed so I didn't have to hear about his moral allergy to pro bono work. Now I snap a quick succession of shots of the band—the frontwoman knows exactly how to present for maximum visual impact in her billowing white dress—then swing my camera around to the crowd. It's generationally diverse, a testament to the enduring power of Jeff Buckley's music. My lens finds more scenes than it can capture, and I wonder if there isn't something more to this show than a remembrance. If maybe this night could shake me out of my artistic stasis. Inspire my next long-term project. Keep me from feeling perpetually unmoored.

When the set ends, I make my way to Emme, who dutifully returned to our original spot after she came back from the bathroom.

Something is wrong. I can see it in her rigid posture, her crossed arms, the defiant set of her mouth. In a matter of milliseconds, using the part of my brain that defies language or logic, I calculate that she isn't physically harmed, and she's not particularly *sad*. She's angry.

"OK." I finally reach Emme through the thick crowd. "Tell me what happened."

She shrugs, dropping her arms to her sides with a dramatic huff. "It's nothing. Just a girl while I was in line for the bathroom."

I feel every fight-or-flight muscle in my body tense, ready to tear apart whoever upset her like this. I flash back to the bout of bullying she faced in middle school before her eclectic interests—manga! calligraphy! collecting vintage subway tokens!—made her categorically cool at her artsy high school.

I take a breath. "What happened?"

With the side of her hand, Emme brushes nonexistent hair from her forehead—her signature pissed-off move. "So I was waiting in line for the bathroom for, like, five million years, and I have never needed to pee so badly in my life—like, the pee was practically leaking out of me—and when I was finally next in line, this girl on a FaceTime call—on speaker, by the way!—brushes right past me and gets into the next open stall before I can. And then she, like, hogs the sink forever, just yapping on her phone. I just get *so mad* when people are so presumptuous. I mean, who does she think she is? Just because she was fucking—sorry—insanely gorgeous with, like, the shiniest hair I have ever seen, *and* she was wearing that miniskirt I've been trying to find, you know the micro one with all the buckles on it? And she also smelled amazing, so I guess she thinks she deserves to pee before the rest of us? I can't stand it." Then, "I don't even think she's from here." The hardest-hitting diss in Emme's arsenal.

"Did you say anything to her?"

"No. And I'm mad about that too. I wish I'd stood up for myself. I just felt really shy all of a sudden."

Empathy spears through me. I know exactly how she feels.

"Try not to be so hard on yourself," I say. "We all have moments when we wish we'd handled things differently."

A little smirk breaks across Emme's face that reminds me of the purple devil emoji. Emme wears it when she's about to say something she knows I won't like.

"You're referring to Dad stuff, aren't you?"

"No, Emme Jade. I'm not referring to Dad stuff."

I'm not *only* referring to Dad stuff.

Since my split with James, I've tried to protect Emme from the extent to which he neglected me, tossed my feelings aside. Didn't consider what I did, said, or thought, let alone care about those things. Or just how long I let his behavior slide, until I became hardened to his hardness, indifferent to his indifference. Until I lost myself so completely that I reached a breaking point.

James loves Emme, but as Emme gets older, his perpetual absence speaks for itself. She doesn't need me to be her translator.

Now I loop my arm through hers, grateful that she's not the kind of teen who's mortified by public shows of affection from her mother, and direct our attention back to the show. The musical acts are now over, and a former waiter at Sin-é, who was also a close friend of Jeff Buckley's, has taken to the stage to reflect on the musician's legacy and his outsized influence. And to remind the crowd to tip their bartenders generously.

Afterward, we slowly filter out to the street. All I want to do right now is get a big bowl of ramen, pop a melatonin, and crawl into bed. My soul may still feel like it's twenty-two, but my back does not.

The June air is balmy and supple. I've lived my entire life in New York City, but I'll never get over the miracle of stepping outside and being met with warm air. Summer is when the city shows its soft center.

We turn toward home, but Emme suddenly grabs my arm.

She freezes in place, her eyes baby-doll-wide, like she's seen a ghost.

"That's her," she says. "That's the bitch—sorry—the *shockingly entitled young woman* who cut me in line for the bathroom."

I follow where she points down the block, toward the fluorescent lights of the movie theater on Third Avenue. There, I see a girl with, indeed, remarkably long, shiny chestnut hair, wearing one of the shortest skirts I've seen in my life. Yes, I recognize this miniskirt Emme has attempted to hunt down. The girl is scrolling through her phone, pinching and pulling her fingers apart on the screen.

I'm about to tell Emme to shake it off, that we can talk more about it over dinner, when I notice something else.

Standing next to the girl is a tall dark-haired man.

The girl leans in to show him something on her phone. When the man tugs a pair of reading glasses out of his shirt pocket, I can't stop looking at the way his shoulders shift beneath his khaki-green chore coat.

Recognition lances through me.

Emme isn't the one who's seeing a ghost.

I am.

VII

The ghost's face is a little more bronzed than I remember, with a sprinkling of fine lines around his eyes and mouth earned from decades of expression, softened beneath the smoggy LA sun. Under the too-bright lights of the movie theater, I can see that his hair is still thick, still mostly oil-spill black, but a little shorter now, with flecks of salt and pepper along the temples.

Time has been good to this ghost. Maddeningly good. He looks better now, even, than when I knew him first.

And the ghost is looking at me too. Looking like he, too, is seeing some spectral something that can't possibly be real.

I can't help what happens next: I take Emme's hand and walk—no, I *drift*—toward where he stands, still magnetized by the pull of him. Somewhere in the distance, I hear my daughter protest-panic. *Please don't make me confront her in public*, I think I hear her say. I give her hand a squeeze, trying to reassure her that this is not about to be a teachable moment for her.

It's only when I'm face-to-face with him that I realize that I have brought myself over here, clutching my daughter's hand like a life raft, and that I should probably say something.

And that what I'd known in my gut was true.

It's Reid.

I might be shocked, but I'm not entirely surprised to see him here. A small part of me hoped that Reid might be at this show. Hoped it despite the fact the occasional furtive, wine-fueled Google searches over the past however-many years confirmed that he still lives in LA, where he's now a successful screenwriter. I had chastised myself for such a quixotic line of thinking, then remembered what my therapist said about my tendency toward an unkind inner monologue: that I would never talk to my daughter the way I talk to myself. I tried to give myself some grace for imagining a romantic future for myself.

As Blondie says, dreaming is free.

Now the smile that breaks across Reid's face alleviates any anxiety I'd had about whether he'd be happy to see me. Whether he would even recognize me.

It's the same smile I once loved: upside-down, like a shrug.

His eyes scan my face, and I don't even have it in me to feel concerned about what he sees there, to consider all the ways I've changed since he saw me last. My hair still falls in long waves, though hints of silver now weave between the dark blond. The remainders of the baby fat that clung to my cheekbones dissolved decades ago. And despite the retinol, the red-light therapy masks, the collagen supplements and medical-grade tinctures, a feathering of fine lines fan across the corners of my eyes and sit contentedly between my brows.

But before either one of us can break this increasingly long silence, Emme interjects, "I saw you in the bathroom, right?"

My gaze falters to the girl standing beside Reid. She looks to be a year or two older than Emme. It becomes instantly clear to me that this is Reid's daughter. They don't look alike, exactly, but I can see him in the arrangement of her features, like glimpsing the silhouette of a person from behind a silk screen. She is ethereally beautiful, an Instagram filter in real life. Her skin is milky, poreless, luminescent along the bridge of her nose and the corners of her almond-shaped eyes, which are the same almost-black color as her hair.

Her mother must be a showstopper, I think.

Momentarily, I marvel at the fact that Reid has a daughter. And then I lose my mind and think, *Isn't he too young to have a teenager?*

Beside me, Emme drops my hand and straightens her posture.

To Reid's daughter, she's saying, "Have you ever heard of the concept of a line?"

My eyes briefly catch on Reid's again, and in that look between us, we have an entire conversation: *Yes, this is me, and yes, this is really happening, and how much time has passed? And what are you doing here? And is this your daughter? And are they about to have a fight right now?*

We drag our gazes away from each other when Reid's daughter responds. She looks genuinely confused, a jut of her lip, and then, all at once, clarity breaks across her features like sunshine.

There it is, I think. *There's Reid.*

"Oh my god, that was you," Reid's daughter says. "I'm sorry. I was distracted by my friend, and I was literally about to pee myself, and I just—"

"Is this your dad?" Emme cuts in.

Quickly, I turn to Emme, unsure whether I want to warn her about her insolence or applaud her for her chutzpah.

Then Reid responds. "I'm her dad, yes," he says, "but I'm not going to apologize on behalf of my daughter. Gracie has to do that for herself."

That voice. That goddamn voice. It's even deeper now, with the barest hint of grit, but it's still the voice that had my underwear around my ankles in an instant.

"I'm sorry," Gracie says. "It was a shitty thing to do. I honestly didn't realize there was a line until I got out of the stall. When you gotta go, you gotta go."

"I mean, when you gotta go, you gotta wait until other people who gotta go who got there first go. You know?" Emme snips back. I muster every ounce of restraint to stop myself from telling her to take it easy, to spare me the awkwardness. Then to Reid, she says, "And you need to get her some AirPods. You can't take personal calls at a fucking—" Emme turns to me, pink cheeked "—sorry, at a very loud, very public concert!"

Gracie takes Emme's castigation in stride. "Yeah, sorry about that. My headphones were dead, but my best friend is obsessed with the nineties and wanted to see some of the show. I couldn't leave her hanging like that."

Emme frowns, but she's seemingly appeased by this explanation: She, too, is obsessed with the nineties, treating the decade with the same idealized fascination with which I imagined my parents' youths in the sixties. It's not uncommon for her to come to me with logistical, borderline anthropological questions about the preinternet era: What did you do if you didn't know the answer to something? (You asked someone.) What if you got lost somewhere? (You asked someone.) But seriously, what if you needed the answer to something and no one around you knew the answer either? (You accepted the not-knowing and moved on with your life.)

"Understood," Emme says now.

Confrontation over, the four of us stand in silence for a moment. But Reid is still looking at me. Like *that*.

"Lili," he says at last.

"Reid," I say back.

Our names are the spell that breaks the dream. I feel crazy then, the dam of self-control utterly broken, and I start to laugh.

Reid joins me, a big, bold laugh that's exactly as easy as I remember it.

Our daughters just stand there, jaws agape, clearly in shock.

When we calm down, Gracie says, "You know each other?" She points a sharp shell-pink nail between us.

"We . . . yeah," Reid says.

I run a finger underneath my eye, cleaning up my smudged mascara. Emme looks horrified—by my sudden hysteria or by a past life she doesn't yet know about, I'm not sure. But I know I need to tread lightly here.

"We used to be friends," I tell the girls.

Over Gracie's head, Reid gives me a semiamused look. *Is* that *what we were?*

"It was a long time ago," I add.

"I mean, it wasn't *that* long ago," Reid says.

"The MetroCard wasn't even invented yet," I say. "That's how long ago it was."

"A MetroCard is how you get into the subway," Emme says to Gracie. I know she's working on asserting herself, but I don't love the condescension. Something to contend with later.

"Mm-hmm," Gracie says. "I gathered that."

OK, then. Confrontation not entirely over.

Reid and I share a look that lands somewhere between alarm and resignation. This, we both know, is what it's like to raise a teenage girl.

For a moment, I wonder what it would be like to co-parent with him. This is not an unfamiliar thought. Sometimes, in the throes of my unhappiness with James, my mind would drift to Reid, to what might have been had he stayed in New York and things had worked out between us. I'd told myself he would have been supportive, encouraging, and loyal. To Emme—I could never imagine my daughter being anyone but Emme, even with a different father—he would have been patient and endlessly kind.

Now I get to see it for real. Unconsciously, his hand brushes the back of Gracie's head in a protective motion. The sweetness almost breaks my soul in half.

I need to regain control over this situation. To get a handle on what is real, even though reality admittedly feels tenuous.

Trying to play it cool, I ask, "What are you two up to now?"

Reid nods toward Gracie's phone. "We were finding a place to grab a bite. Gracie wants to try this vegan soul food spot on Seventh Street—"

"Cadence?" Emme says.

Reid points a finger-gun at her, a move that would've been pocket-protector-dad nerdy had anyone other than him done it. "That's the one. But I'm trying to convince her to go to John's of 12th Street. I saw they have a whole plant-based menu going on."

"You're vegetarian?" Emme asks Gracie.

"Vegan," Gracie says. Emme makes a surprised humming noise in approval. "But TikTok says there's a line, and if I don't eat something in the next ten minutes, I will scream."

Somehow, I believe her. "I know the owner," I say. It's a little pathetic, the *ding* of pride I feel when Reid gives me an impressed look. "My mom babysat for him when she was a teenager. I can get us a table, if you don't mind us joining you."

Emme and I have always been close, but since the divorce, and then lockdown, she and I have developed an uncanny ability to communicate silently. Now the look I give her is a question: *Are you OK with this?*

The look she gives me back says, *I'd rather not, but I'm hungry, so I'll do it.*

Then I say, *I love you. You're the coolest.*

Reid sticks his hands in his pockets and nods at me slowly. "Interesting," he says. "I don't remember you taking advantage of your connections when we were . . ."

He doesn't finish that sentence. When we were . . . what? Sleeping together? Obsessed? Falling in love?

"I'll make up for it now," I say.

I see Gracie and Emme trade a look like *What the* fuck *is going on between our parents?*

Then Reid grins at me. I notice the smallest chip in his front tooth. That didn't exist thirty years ago.

"OK, then," he says. "Let's see what's happening on Twelfth Street."

VIII

As soon as we sit down, I know this was a bad idea.

When we walked into the old-school Italian restaurant, the owner's son, Massimo, greeted me with a hug and a double kiss, asked after my parents, then looked at the hostess and touched his finger to his nose, the sign of a free dessert or bottle of wine. And then he deposited us at our table, a cozy booth in the back, and took all his warmth and gregariousness with him.

Now the four of us consider our menus in silence. A jazzy rendition of Shania Twain's "You're Still the One" plays over the speakers. At the six-top next to us, a compendium of eclectic older women—lots of velvet scarves and jawbreaker jewelry—gossip about someone named Janice. At the table behind us, a young woman in a slicked-back bun and twisted gold earrings reads Eve Babitz's *Sex and Rage*.

I clock all this because nothing is happening at our table. Or, a lot is happening at our table, but all of it subterranean. The tension between the girls is still pulled taut. I keep trying to catch Reid's eye, but he won't meet my gaze.

A barrage of unwanted thoughts comes tumbling in.

Did he only take up my invitation out of his unfailing politeness? Seeing me now, in middle age, is he looking back at our time less rosily?

Then he rests his arm over the back of the booth, behind where Gracie sits, and it clicks: He's protecting his daughter's feelings and waiting to make sure she's OK with this admittedly odd situation. I'm ashamed that I considered any other alternative.

Then a waiter stops at our table and asks if we'd like something to drink.

"Yes," Reid and I say simultaneously, with feeling.

The waiter laughs. We laugh. We order a bottle of Chianti. The girls continue to icily consider their menus and avoid eye contact with their respective parents. But it's something.

There is so much I want to ask Reid, but I start with the most obvious question. "What were you two doing at the show?"

I watch Reid glance at Gracie before he responds. From my vantage, she remains expressionless, but clearly Reid saw something that loosens him up a little bit.

"Gracie came across the announcement on Instagram." Reid gives her a playful look. "She and I are in town until Tuesday—she finally wore me down and got me to take her on a tour of NYU."

"You have a problem with NYU?" I say in mock defense. To Gracie, I clarify, "It's my alma mater."

Her expression remains intelligently blank, revealing nothing to display that she has received this information.

"I do have a problem with it, actually," Reid says. "It's three thousand miles away from me and her aunt Cat."

At this, I expect Gracie to roll her eyes. Emme certainly would. But instead, she gives her dad a small, tender smile. It seems the protectiveness goes both ways.

"Cat, my god," I say, my voice wistful.

"The one and only," Reid says. "She's head of A&R at a label now, if you can believe it. Actually, that Jeff Buckley show was kind of an epiphany for her. Something about your confusion over whether we worked in the music industry . . . it made her believe that she could actually do something like that. She ended up coming out to LA a couple weeks after I went back. Started in the mailroom at Epitaph Records, broke some cult bands, and worked her way into a major label."

I laugh, remembering how naive I had been to think two scrappy kids were corporate bigwigs. That was so like me then, though. To believe that everyone other than me had some secret well of power and authority that I could never tap into myself. Eventually, I discovered that power isn't bestowed by a magic elixir: It's earned through the choices you make.

"She's been really good to Gracie." Reid gives Gracie another look, suffused with a meaning only she could understand. "Basically helped me raise her."

"Childless rich aunts make good surrogate moms," Gracie deadpans.

I may not know Gracie, but I do know when a kid is trying to hide their pain with humor. Emme did it during the bullying years and still does it, sometimes, in regards to James and me.

Reid doesn't interject with anything about Gracie's actual mother, which also gives context to his bare left ring finger. I don't know how she might figure here, but the explanation can't be easy.

Reid clears his throat, like he knows he's gone too far, then smoothly changes the subject.

"Emme, what'd you think of the show? Are you a Jeff Buckley fan too?"

Emme's been mostly quiet, absorbed in pretending to study the menu—I know she's getting the seitan parmigiana, but she's putting on a good show—and now she brightens, sitting forward in her seat. "I loved it," she said. "The way Ray Bull made 'Mojo Pin' sound like an Elton John piano ballad? Genius. It gave me chills."

"I agree," Reid says. "I don't know if they'd rescind my legit card for saying this, but that cover might be better than the original. *Might* be."

"Don't say *legit card*," Gracie says. "And don't blaspheme my namesake."

Gracie. As in *Grace*, Jeff Buckley's only studio album. Reid notices my delayed epiphany.

"Her mother's favorite album," he explains. "Mine too. But I think you already knew that."

When he turns his attention back to Gracie, I use the opportunity to study him a little more closely. The way he sits back against the booth, an ankle thrown easily over a knee; how his T-shirt—the rumpled, tissue-thin material that is the calling card of a certain egregiously expensive basics brand—highlights his broad chest and shoulders.

Again and again, I'm struck with a sense of unreality. This is Reid, exactly as I knew him, and he is also a different person entirely, with a daunting vault of memories and experiences that are completely hidden from me.

And I wonder whether he's considering me the same way.

But I keep shaking off the existential crisis to enjoy our conversation, which starts to pick up once our wine and food arrive. When the topic turns to last month's Met Gala red carpet, Gracie and Emme even begin to address each other directly. Phoebe Bridgers's Tory Burch look was a mutual favorite. So was Doja Cat's campy glam kitty costume.

At one point, in the midst of talk about the potential schools the girls are each interested in (Gracie, who's a rising senior, wants to go into premed), Gracie interrupts herself.

"Hang on," she says. She points that razor-sharp nail at me. A silver bow charm dangles off the tip. "You said you know Aunt Cat?"

"I did." I mentally attempt to retrace the conversation and remember what I revealed. We haven't been talking about Cat since we sat down. Gracie must have been turning this over in her mind since then. Did I reveal something I shouldn't have or cross a line I didn't know existed?

Then Gracie swings her finger at her dad. "And you

said *that* Jeff Buckley show?" He nods. Gracie turns back to me. "You were there?"

I nod. "Sin-é, 1993. That's where your dad and I met." Maybe I've had too much wine, but now I give Reid a brazen, challenging look. "Caught him by the coattails before he left New York."

Reid laughs, low in his throat. "Sure did."

Gracie nods her head slowly. Then she drops her napkin on the table and stands. Abruptly, she says, "I'm gonna go to the bathroom. Emme, can you show me where it is?"

Emme, midbite, gives her a look like *Me? Now?*

Gracie arches a perfectly groomed eyebrow. *Now. You.*

I'm just as confused as Emme is—clearly, Gracie is up to something. I'm embarrassed to admit that I'm slightly afraid of what that might be.

But with the girls gone, the energy shifts. It is just the two of us, for the first time in twenty years. Reid's shoulders drop a few inches. I smooth a hand through my hair. In the newfound quiet, a sense of intimacy blooms between us, like we can assume a freedom of conversation unbound by a duty to protect our children's emotions. Be one person talking to another person, with no agenda other than connection.

Now Reid gestures to my camera, occupying the space between me and Emme on our side of the booth like a mechanical, alien baby. "Glad to see your minor won out."

I laugh. "I can't believe you remember that."

"I also remember we got you that five-hundred-pound Shakespeare collection for one of your lit classes. Pretty sure carrying that thing back to your place permanently fucked up my shoulder."

My face flushes. Does that mean he also remembers when he stuck his thumb in my mouth in the basement of the bookstore?

"I think those books are still at my parents' house. After graduation, I took a stab as an editorial assistant at a publishing house, but I felt like an impostor. Actually, it was Emme's dad who convinced me to quit and try to make the photography thing work." Before he can ask, I say, "We divorced six years ago."

Reid is leaning forward across the table, a crease between his brows. I haven't forgotten how good it feels to be on the receiving end of his attention, and I feel a desire to pick up my camera and capture this scene—how the dancing flame on the table throws delicate shadows across his features, sending a single perfect starburst of light into the center of his amber-flecked eyes.

"I'm sorry," Reid says. "What happened there? With the marriage?"

"Kind of a classic he-was-married-to-his-work situation, though the real red flag was that I was starting to dread the moment he walked through the door. We'd drifted apart so much that I hardly knew who he was anymore, and honestly, I wasn't that interested in figuring out who the new version was. And he certainly wasn't interested in me." I stop myself, caught off guard by my uncharacteristic candor. *You* knew *Reid, you don't* know *Reid*, I remind myself. I sigh, drain the last of my wine.

"He wasn't cut out to be a husband, but he tries to be a good dad."

Reid tops up our glasses. "He *tries*?"

I hesitate for a moment, unsure how deeply I want to get into this right now. So I just say, "James is a trauma surgeon. He has a habit of putting his work above parenting. Last weekend, there was a car crash on the LIE, and he canceled plans he'd made with Emme to see a Broadway show. When lives are on the line, it's hard to argue—he always has the moral high ground. But he's not *the only* trauma surgeon in New York City."

Reid shakes his head. "Can't imagine bailing on Gracie." Then he shrugs. "That said, I'm certainly not saving lives with my work."

I nod. "Most of us aren't. So I struggle with this push and pull with him. It feels unethical—fucked—to fault the guy for literally saving lives. But at the same time . . . there's a bit of a god complex, and the way Emme's face falls when her dad blows her off is seared into my brain."

"Yeah, one of my main goals in life is to make Gracie *not* make that face whenever possible. I will never forget the time I wouldn't let her get a pet goldfish and she looked at me like . . . I don't know. Like I'd squashed it with my bare hands in front of her. It's tricky. You want to make sure they're prepared for the world without crushing their spirit."

"I'm still trying to figure out that dance between protection and . . . overprotection." I look down and realize my glass is almost empty again.

"It seems like you've found the right balance with Emme."

A rush of warmth floods in my chest. A compliment from Reid lands harder than most.

"Did you get her the goldfish?" I ask.

"I got her three."

"Three goldfish!"

"Leonardo, Donatello, and Michelangelo."

"As in the Renaissance artists?"

"As in the Ninja Turtles."

"What about Raphael?"

He leans over the table. It's a thrill to be this close to him, to smell the musk of his shirt, to see the deeper tan along his nose and cheeks.

"Gracie," he drops his voice, goes serious, "did not like Raphael."

I laugh. "And what about you? How is that nonlife-saving work going?"

I know what the answer is. I've skimmed the headlines about him, announcing his major deals, his even more major wins. My experience of those moments was a rush of pride, followed quickly by regret. I always stopped short of clicking into the links, afraid of losing my footing, getting caught in the storm of complicated, conflicting emotions. Catching those flashes of his life had always felt illicit, like peering through a peephole.

But now, sitting with Reid himself, it feels . . . easy. I'm eager to hear him talk about his success. I'm walking right through a door, which he's opened for me with a smile.

"Work is going well," he says, sitting back in his chair again. It's an understatement, and I'm happy to find that Reid's ego has remained in check. "Somehow still a screenwriter." He runs a hand through his hair. "All this gray? Wouldn't exist if I'd found something else to do with my life."

"It's really amazing, Reid." I let myself acknowledge that his career isn't news to me.

"What's amazing is that we're both doing the things we set out to do."

"Eh," I shrug. "If it were up to me, I'd be shooting fewer ads and more fine art. Turns out you can't send a kid to college off the kind of photos I took tonight."

"Either way, you're making a living off something you love. That doesn't happen very often, for our generation."

"It is very Gen Z of us, isn't it? Actually following our dreams?" I joke. He laughs. "OK, this may be un-Hollywood of me to say, but I saw that you won an Oscar for *Mask of Sin*."

He drops his head slightly, like he's trying to deflect this confrontation with his own success. "Get Amy Adams to play the proprietor of a gambling den and you kind of can't lose." He takes a swig of his wine. "I still haven't managed not to feel mortified when I talk about my writing, even thirty years in. But yes, you're right. That was un-Hollywood of you."

"Then teach me how to be Hollywood," I say. There's an unmistakable hint of flirtation in my tone.

He leans into it. He looks up at me through a crinkled

brow, a devilish glint in his eyes. "Rules are pretty simple. You would pretend you have no idea who I am, gradually befriend me, invite me to a casual dinner with other people in the industry, including people I've worked with previously, pretend to be surprised when the topic of awards comes up, and then, after a span of three-to-six months, ask me for a favor that you'd had planned from the beginning."

I look him dead in the eye. "I have never heard of you in my life."

"You're getting the hang of it."

"Well, too bad, I'm proud of you. You're really doing the thing."

He sits back. When he smiles now, I notice something behind his eyes that I hadn't before now. And never did, thirty years ago. It's pain.

"I suppose I am," Reid says. "I could never have imagined this for myself. The people I've gotten to work with, the movies I've been able to make . . . But a lot of it—work, life—is not what I thought it would be."

Lightly, I touch his hand where it rests on the table, trying to convey to him how much I get it. My life, too, has taken some unpredictable turns. He looks down, as if to consider whether he wants us to be in physical contact. I begin to pull away, to apologize for crossing the boundary, but he flips his palm up, as if to hold me in place.

"Lili," he says. "I feel like I should tell you—"

And that's when Emme and Gracie come back to the table. Quickly, we pull our hands away and innocently pick our forks up again.

When they sit back down, Gracie announces, "Emme's gonna show me around the NYU campus tomorrow."

Reid and I raise our eyebrows at each other. Clearly, he is just as in the dark as I am about whatever is going on between these two.

I look over at Emme, who's now sporting a slick of shimmering chocolate-brown lip gloss. It's the same one Gracie is wearing. Such is the magic of the girls' bathroom.

Emme throws up her hands. "I've lived on Waverly my entire life."

"Well, I think that's a great idea," Reid says. "You can show her the insider spots."

"Don't say *insider spots*," Gracie says.

Emme claps her hands together. "Yeah! I'll come up with an itinerary. But, like, a cool one." Then she shoots a look between Reid and me. "Why don't you guys go do something too?"

"Oh," I say. After that moment of hesitation, whatever Reid felt the need to caution me about . . . I'm not so sure he wants to see me again. And depending on whatever it is he wanted to share, I'm not entirely sure it would be a good thing to see him again either. It's clear that he's no longer with Gracie's mother, but that doesn't mean he's not in a relationship. Actually, I find it hard to believe he's not. How couldn't he be, with that face and that voice and that kindness?

My cheeks heat as it hits me: I still have a giant crush on this man.

"Dad, do not use the work excuse," Gracie says. "You

need to learn how to have fun." She offers me the barest glance. "And Lili seems fun."

"Lili *is* fun," Reid says. "I can confirm."

I can't quite read the expression on his face then. Is it an apology? A warning?

"Are you free tomorrow?" he asks me. He looks . . . like someone who wasn't just put up to this by his kid.

Technically, I'm not really free. I have to review and edit the images from tonight to send to the client, call the plumber about the terminally low water pressure in my bathroom sink, take Emme's dress to the tailor, schedule her dentist appointment . . .

But it's been a really long time since I've had a crush.

"I'm wide open," I say.

"OK, let's talk about this," I say. Emme and I are walking home from the restaurant, where we left Reid and Gracie to grab an Uber back to their hotel uptown. In a shocking twist, Gracie and Emme hugged goodbye.

"Talk about what?" Emme responds.

I gesture behind me, conveying the very recent past. "Dinner. Reid. All of it. How do you feel about it?"

Emme hikes her canvas bag up her shoulder. I don't know what she has in there, but it looks heavy. "Should I feel some type of way about it?"

So she's playing coy. She does this when she wants to skirt an issue, or she wants *me* to admit I'm skirting an issue.

I have to be more direct. That's the rule of the game.

"I'm guessing you gathered that Reid and I dated. It was right before my junior year of college. I don't even know if you could call it a relationship—we knew each other for about a week. It was short, but I had very strong feelings for him."

"A situationship," Emme offers.

"Yes, that. I know it's probably weird to see me . . . interact with a man who's not your dad."

I've only gone on a handful of dates since the divorce, mainly at the urging of Nisha and my therapist, who hold eerily similar opinions about how I need to push past my romantic comfort zone. How I need to stop putting my own needs and desires on hold until Emme leaves home. The ways in which I've supplanted those needs and desires entirely with things that require little emotional risk. None of my previous dates were terrible, but none of them felt worth making things more complicated for Emme. James was already a pro at that.

Now Emme shrugs. "I mean, OK, fine, it's a little weird." We pause at the carts of bargain books outside the Strand. Emme thumbs through a row of travel books, all of them at least fifteen years out of date. "Do you still like him?"

"I liked him thirty years ago. But people change. I don't really know who he is now."

"But you're looking forward to spending more time with him. Tomorrow, I mean."

Before we left the restaurant, Reid and I made a plan to meet for lunch at a bistro in the West Village, a decision that pleased all four of us. It was far enough away from where the girls would be that we wouldn't risk running into them but close enough to make Reid feel comfortable. A break-in-case-of-emergency thing.

Emme is flipping through the books more quickly now, distracted or anxious. I put a hand on her arm, nudging her to look at me. "Emme. If you don't feel comfortable with me seeing Reid again, I won't do it, and I won't have any regrets about it. You will always come first. OK?"

Emme releases a labored sigh, like I'm not getting something. "I like Reid, Mom. He paid attention to you when you talked. He actually asked you questions, and then he listened when you answered." My heart fractures. "I like Gracie too. She wants people to think she's a bitch, but she's actually a very thoughtful person. You know, she only supports cruelty-free beauty brands. And she really cares about her dad."

"I also like Gracie. And I like that Reid asked you questions too."

"Yeah, he didn't treat me like a seen-and-not-heard kind of kid." She looks at me earnestly. "You have to go," she says, but then pauses, like she's cutting herself off. I pluck the book from her hand—a brick-sized, age-softened anthology of vampire literature.

"I'll get this for you if you tell me what else is on your mind," I say. One thing it took me too long to learn about parenting is the power of a well-timed bribe.

She ruminates for a moment. "Can I get a hardcover too?"

"Absolutely."

"I want you to be careful."

Alarm bells. "Careful how?"

"Careful like, I don't want your heart to get stomped on again." She waves a hand toward me. "The postdivorce-sad-mom thing sucked. I honestly don't want either of us to go through that again."

It never ceases to be surprising, the labor of creating a person, followed by the miracle of watching them morph, slowly and also all at once, into someone you have never met. And the delicious pain of your heart expanding beyond its known borders each time you encounter a new iteration.

This is an Emme I haven't yet known, protective and wise. But I still need to guard her feelings more than she needs to guard mine.

"That won't happen," I say. "I can promise you that."

Another thing I've learned about parenting: the power of a white lie.

IX

I arrive at the restaurant with time to spare, needing a moment to settle in before Reid appears. The hostess leads me to a sunny table tucked into the corner, and I order a peppermint tea. My body is already electric, and more caffeine would tip me over the edge. I'm surprised by the jangle of my nerves. I keep reminding myself that I was in this man's presence just last night. That Reid and I maybe even loved each other once, that he's not some stranger whose approval I'm courting. That he has, in fact, seen me naked. Though my pulse only kicks up more in response to all of it.

When Reid walks in, his eyes sweep the room until they find me. He greets me with a smile, warm and familiar, and it's like the light pulses through the window with an even gentler glow. He looks good in a white cotton T-shirt that brings out the bronze of his skin. The thin silver chain of a necklace is barely visible above the neckline. I wish I had my camera with me, and that it wouldn't be strange to ask to take his portrait.

Maybe we can work up to that.

Reid leans down for a brief hug, just long enough that I can breathe in his scent. My heartbeat ratchets up again.

"That color's beautiful on you," he says, settling into his chair.

"Thank you." Heat climbs my neck, though of course I deliberately chose this outfit: a gossamer, blue-gray top with a plunging neckline, and a pair of high-waisted flared jeans that, according to Nisha, J.Lo also owns. (One thing I love about my brilliant biochemical engineer friend: She still has a print subscription to *Us Weekly*.) It's been a long time since I've dressed for anyone other than myself, and I've forgotten this particular thrill—the way the right clothes can summon exactly the words I want to hear.

The waitress comes to take Reid's drink order—an Americano, with a splash of milk—and after she leaves, we regard each other quietly for a handful of seconds. The silence isn't uncomfortable; there's a giddiness to it that I recognize from long ago. A pocket of possibility opens up between us, and suddenly we're twenty and twenty-two again, recognizing each other as a well of potential and adventure.

"This is weird, right?" I finally ask, breaking the silence.

"So fucking weird," Reid agrees, laughing.

"Good. Now we can actually talk."

When he smiles, I notice the tiny chip in his front tooth, the one that wasn't there when we were young.

"Where did that come from?" I tap my own tooth.

"Ah. So you did notice it." His cheeks redden, like he's ashamed for having wondered. "Happened the summer I met you, actually, about a week after I got back to LA. I was skateboarding with a friend in Echo Park—"

"Hang on. You skateboarded?"

"Of course I did." Reid gestures vaguely at himself. "Southern California kid." His gaze scans over me. "Why? You like that?"

"Of course I do." I wave my hand in front of my own face. "New York City kid."

"Well, my skating days pretty much ended after that. That neighborhood has some ridiculously steep streets, just these relentless drops, and my shithead friend dared me to skate one of the really hellish ones. I'm lucky I didn't crack my skull open."

I cock my head, remembering how I'd needed to coax him out onto the fire escape at that party on East Fifth Street. "I thought you were afraid of heights."

Reid tilts his head too, like he's also remembering that moment. "I hate them, but I was feeling pretty reckless that day." He looks at me challengingly. "Got the job but lost the girl."

"Hm," I say. "I can't imagine why she would've let you go."

"Maybe if she hadn't, I'd still have the rest of my tooth."

"But you wouldn't look so ruggedly handsome."

His gaze unhurriedly travels my face before dropping to my mouth, stays there a beat too long. My brain short-circuits, and I'm hit with a memory of his mouth on my skin, the way his breath alone made me needy and liquid.

From the wicked curve of his lips, I think he's remembering the same. I came apart so easily beneath his hands.

Then I feel my phone buzz in my bag, breaking the

tension between us. *Please*, I think, *do not ring again. Let me stay in this moment, let me pretend there's nothing else in my world to attend to.*

It buzzes insistently.

"I'm sorry," I say, reaching down to grab it. "This could be Emme."

Reid clears his throat, a verbal bucket of cold water thrown onto himself. "No need to apologize."

But when I check the missed call, it's not Emme. It's my dad.

Dread washes over me, as it always does when my parents call unexpectedly. A year ago, my father miraculously survived a widow-maker heart attack, thanks in part to James, who immediately called in a favor with his hospital's best interventional cardiologist. He's managed to make a full recovery physically, and emotionally too. For this, I have his immigrant's mindset to thank: You make a survival, you move on.

But the experience left me traumatized.

"Everything OK?" Reid asks.

"I'm . . . actually not sure. It's my dad. He's not usually the type to spring a random call on me."

He shoos me. "Go. Call him back. Believe me, I get the sandwich generation routine. Call your dad."

I dial on my way to the restroom. My dad picks up after a single ring, which means he's been waiting by the phone.

"You OK?" I ask in greeting. I keep my tone light to hide the worry, but I know my dad can see right through me.

"Sweetheart, I'm fine," he assures me in his broad

Brooklynese accent. I flinch when I hear a groan on the other end. "I'm just getting out of my club chair. You know how deep this thing is? You sink right down into the bowels of the earth. I can practically smell the subway stink from here."

"You know they make better chairs now."

"No, no. I like my chair to hell."

"Your prerogative." Satisfied that he's not in any immediate danger, I glance in the mirror, lean in closer, and touch up my lip gloss.

"So Lili-bean," he says. "Any chance you want to schlep uptown this afternoon?"

My lip gloss hovers over my mouth. My dad rarely makes last-minute demands on my time.

"I'm at lunch with a friend," I say.

"Oh, good, good. Go, enjoy yourself. I'll call you later."

I know he's relieved that he doesn't have to follow through on asking me for help, but I won't let him run. "Dad. What do you need?"

"Eh, it's nothing. I'm just getting some paperwork together. Streamlining, organizing, et cetera. Your mother thinks it was a good idea you had, to start paying our bills on the computer. I tell her we're fine, ConEd will still accept a paper check, but she wants to make it easier for us. So, you know. I thought maybe you could help me with this."

Before the heart attack, my father never talked about what might happen when he and my mother decline, or when one of them passes. But once he was back on his feet, he had me sign a power of attorney for both him and my mom, updated his will, and informed me, with his characteristic no-nonsense approach, that he bought plots for himself and my mom at Beth Olam Cemetery—at a discount, no less. They run a two-for-one special.

It was my suggestion to set up all their recurring payments on autopay, just to give them one less thing to think about. And myself, when the time comes that I'll need to take over their finances. But getting him to agree to this has been an uphill battle. This is a man who crawled his way out of Lithuania and came to New York at nine years old without a lick of English. This is a man who still, at eighty-five, reads a book a week and does the Sunday *Times* crossword puzzle in pen. He is not going to give up his independence without a fight.

But today—for reasons known only to him—he is relenting.

"It's fine," I say. "I can leave lunch in a few minutes. I'll be there in half an hour."

I hope that Reid will understand. And then I *know* he will. I remember his devotion to his own mother. That she was one of the reasons why he was resistant to staying in New York.

"No, no, don't cancel on my account. Is Emmela around today? Tell her to come help me. Your mother wants to give her something anyway. Some old purses, I don't know."

"Dad, Emme doesn't even know how to work a landline. She can't help you with this. I'll see you in a bit."

Another groan. "OK, but don't eat too much before

you leave. Your mother went crazy at Zabar's and bought a pound of nova."

When I get back to the table, Reid is reading something intently on his phone, wearing a pair of tortoiseshell glasses. Combined with the slash of stubble along his jaw, they give him a sexy, professorial look.

He takes them off when I sit down and puts his phone away. Concern crosses his expression, and I momentarily lose all my resolve to leave this restaurant.

"My parents are fine. My dad just wanted me to come help him with something. I was thinking about going up to their apartment now, but . . ."

"Damn. I knew I should've listened to Cat when she told me to cover up the gray hair."

I laugh. "Please don't." I sigh and look down at my hands clasped on the table. "My dad asked if I could help him arrange some of his finances, and he is quite possibly the most stubborn man on earth. If I don't do this now, he'll probably never give me the opportunity again. This, today, is my window."

"I'll come help you, then." He says this with casual conviction, as if it's not just the obvious choice but also the *only* choice.

"Reid," I say, laughing harder, "I can't ask you to set up an elderly couple's autopay during your limited time in New York."

"You didn't ask me to set up an elderly couple's autopay during my limited time in New York. I'm telling you that I want to do it."

"I . . ."

He holds up a hand. "Stop questioning this. I want to spend time with you, and I also like being a come-with guy. Just accept it."

"A 'come-with' guy?"

"The *Seinfeld* pilot." I look at him blankly. "Jesus, Lili. And you call yourself a New Yorker?"

Then he waves away my credit card and drops his on the table.

"I'll let Gracie know our plans changed, but I can't show up empty-handed," he says. "Any good bakeries in the neighborhood?"

"You see? It was a good thing I got the extra lox," my mom says.

She nudges the plate of salmon across the table toward Reid. He's already eaten a bagel and a half, like a champ. Now he declines the fish but astutely asks for another scoop of coleslaw.

We're sitting at my parents' sun-drenched kitchen table, beside the curved bay windows that overlook Riverside Park and the sparkling gray-green Hudson beyond. It's a gorgeous early summer day, and my mother has cracked open the window. A sense of satisfaction settles over me, that special *click* of putting everything in its right place. Not only did we set up my parents' electric, credit card, maintenance, and mortgage payments this morning, but we also collected all their login information (which previously my father had scrawled on loose Post-it notes), wrote it out on a single piece of notebook paper, and took a photo of that piece of paper for when it inevitably gets misplaced.

Reid was game throughout this ordeal, though once or twice I noticed him moving to reach for the mouse when my dad stumbled through a step before tethering his patience and calmly walking him through the explanation one more time. And he laughed genuinely at all my father's jokes, including the one about the first Jewish president's inauguration that I personally have heard a minimum of four hundred times. My father rolls this one out first, but only to people he's trying to impress: "See that man at the podium?" the president-elect's mother whispers to the man sitting next to her. "His brother is a *doctor*."

While we holed ourselves up in my father's study—the "computer room," as he still calls it—my mother plied us with coffee and cookies before breaking out her overzealous deli run. She even pulled out a bottle of champagne, which has been sitting in their fridge since their fiftieth wedding anniversary in 2018. I know this because I bought it for them.

Before we arrived, I texted my mom with the least-complicated explanation for the strapping gentleman joining me to help digitize their bills: Reid is an old friend from college, in town from Los Angeles with his daughter.

When we walked in, I noticed my mother do the thing she's always done when confronted with a good-looking man: straighten her posture and gently touch her fingers to her hair, a Jean Seberg–esque pixie cut she's maintained for the past thirty-five years, once butter-blond and now an elegant dove gray.

Then Reid presented to her the box of black-and-white cookies he picked up on the way, and she's been his shadow since.

"Leave the kid alone," my dad says now. In a show of solidarity, he pulls the plate of lox toward him, away from Reid. My mom playfully slaps at his hand.

Reid laughs. "Believe me, I appreciate this. LA has some great delis, but the bagels don't come close."

"It's the water," my mom intones, as if she has come to this conclusion herself, after years of rigorous experimentation. "It's no good out there."

Her eyes narrow, studying Reid intently, generally the precursor to a probing question. I want to swoop in with something, anything, to get the attention off him—*Emme is learning how to make crochet sushi figurines!*—but my mom has decades of practice in the art of extracting information. She cuts in faster than I do.

"So you have a daughter." She innocently busies herself with topping up our glasses.

"I do." Pride radiates even from those two words. "Gracie. She's going into her senior year of high school."

"Gracie's two years older than Emme," I add, reattempting to gain control over this conversation. "She's interested in NYU, so Emme is showing her around the neighborhood today. I know they're going to Washington Square Park, and I think she's taking Gracie to that Thai restaurant on West Third Street? Remember the one we went to after Emme's dance recital a few years ago?"

But my mom would never relinquish her agenda so easily.

"So it's just you and your daughter here?"

Reid takes a long sip of his drink. He nods warmly. "Just me and Gracie, yes. Always just me and Gracie."

My mom lifts an eyebrow. "Divorced?"

"Mom," I warn. Under the table, I graze my hand against Reid's leg, trying to communicate to him that he doesn't have to answer this question.

Even though I desperately want to know.

"It's OK." Reid looks at me briefly, and there's something like an apology in his eyes. Then he turns his gaze back to the table and grips his champagne glass with slightly too much force. "Widower."

The word is a stone, dropped in a bucket. It shatters the levity of the afternoon.

There's a beat of silence. When he looks back up at my mother, his gracious smile is back in place. But I can see the effort it took for him to get there.

This is what he wanted to tell me about last night at dinner, I realize now. I study Reid's face through the lens of this new knowledge. This is the cause of the emotion I noticed stalking the lightness behind his eyes. This is the suffering Gracie scrambled to cover up. This is why Reid wants to keep her so close.

I picture him again as a twenty-two-year-old—all his promise, his gameness, his carefully laid plans and good manners. I see Reid on the fire escape, the fairy lights dancing in his eyes. I want to keep him there.

"Oh, Reid." I gently touch his elbow, and he offers me the smallest smile.

My mother's hand flies to her heart. The gesture is old-fashioned, somehow, an open, unironic demonstration of her sympathy. "That's just terrible," she says. "I'm sorry, honey."

"Thank you, Joan," Reid says. "I am too."

After that, I manage to finally redirect the conversation toward neutral ground, and my parents eagerly follow. My dad tells a story about meeting Edie Sedgwick at a Factory party. ("All I remember is she was wearing a pair of little boy's overalls, with nothing underneath.") My mom brings out a Salvador Dalí statuette, a twisted Christ rendered in eighteen-karat gold, another of her collection's crown jewels. And then Reid trades a story about how, back in the sixties, his chronically late mother had just missed meeting Dalí at one of Frank Zappa's parties in the Canyon. ("That was the last time she was late for anything.")

Eventually, after we finish up the champagne and clear the table, my father recruits Reid to help him fix his printer. "While I have a young person here," he says. "This thing hasn't worked since the Obama administration. The first one."

Reid follows him. "At fifty-two, it's nice to be called young."

After they leave, I load the dishwasher while my mom handwashes the cabbage platters and good knives. ("Never put a wooden handle in the dishwasher," I hear her refrain.)

We're quiet for a while. I know it won't last.

My mom hands me a dish towel and a platter. "Reid is a nice man."

I can't help but laugh at her opening gambit, and she does too.

"He is indeed," I say.

"He's a friend from college, you said? I don't remember ever meeting him."

"You didn't. I didn't know him well enough to introduce you."

She drops a handful of knives onto my dish towel. "And you know him well enough now?"

I pause. It's a good question, and one I've been grappling with since last night. How well do I know Reid? How well did I *ever* know Reid? We only spent a week together, though the depth of our connection never quite squared with the brevity of our . . . whatever it was. And then there was another lifetime's worth of elapsed years.

I think back to when I saw him first, on that hellishly hot day at Sin-é. The way I felt intuitively that I'd encountered him before, that I knew all the tics and quirks and vulnerabilities that hid behind his cool exterior. And I felt that way again when I saw him last night. The distinct . . . *Reid*-ness of him was how I recognized him from a distance, across the deep, wide gulf of time.

I run the dish towel over a knife, then wrap it around the wooden handle and gently press the water from it.

"I know him as well as I possibly can," I say. It's the most honest answer I can give.

"You didn't know his wife died. Don't you think he should have told you sooner? And not in front of your parents?"

"It's . . . complicated." I take a deep breath. "I don't know, Mom. You don't get to our age without collecting some baggage."

My mom puts her hand on mine and squeezes it. Her nails are painted the color of glossy candy apples, as they have been since at least 1985. The big things change, but the small things don't. The small things, I think, are often the most meaningful.

"That man," my mom says, "is in pain."

My heart sinks. There's something about my mom telling me what I already know that makes it even more real. I know she's right. And I know Emme was right last night, when she warned me to guard my heart. Before now, I never would have second-guessed these warnings. I never even would have gotten to a point in my feelings when I would have needed to be warned anyway. I certainly didn't with the handful of men I dated after James and I split.

But none of those men were Reid. There's something about him that calls to something in me, a quiet hum of resonance I'd forgotten I could hear.

I like him. The admission to myself feels dangerous. I like him enough that I'm actually considering poking my head out of the shell I retracted into after the divorce. He's only been back in my life for a matter of hours, but I can already feel myself changing shape, becoming a person who might take calculated risks again.

I open the drawer at my waist and slot the dried-off knives inside. From the office, I hear the labored chug of the printer, followed by the whoop of my dad's laugh.

"I don't know anyone who isn't in pain," I say. "But maybe we don't have to let our pain rule us."

My mom raises a brow in a way that means she's seeing right through me. "I wish you really believed that, sweetheart."

X

"Tell me honestly," I say. "How bad were my parents?"

"What kind of scale are we talking?" Reid asks.

"Classic one to ten."

"Ten being?"

"You're on an unairconditioned plane to Florida. Middle seat, screaming baby behind you, you can't get the WiFi to work, and your TV is broken."

"And what's one?"

"Whatever is your bliss." I shrug. "You tell me."

We cross Waverly, heading into Washington Square Park. Predictably, it is mobbed—it's the first sunny Saturday afternoon in June, which is, as Emme would say, when people get feral. There is something elemental in the energy, the scent of weed and warm pretzels playing on a nostalgic loop, and delicate piles of white and pink cherry blossoms mounding on the pavement. Reid is about to walk underneath the arch—the triumphal, ornate marble portal that stands sentry at the entrance to the park—but I grab hold of his bicep and steer him around it, taking us in the long way.

"Sorry," I say, when he raises an eyebrow at me. "There's this NYU superstition that if you walk directly underneath it, you'll fail your finals. I obviously have no finals left to fail, but it still feels ominous."

"Old habits die hard."

Which is when I realize that I'm still holding on to his arm. I let go, pretending to readjust my bag. I notice Reid shrug a shoulder, like he's acclimating to the lack of my presence there.

"Your parents weren't nearly as bad as you worry they were," Reid continues.

"Even with the third degree?"

Reid laughs. "I can handle two octogenarians."

We wind around the fountain, and I remember the way we walked down the street together before, a tangle of arms and hands, how Reid would sometimes trip over himself when he forced his long legs to meet my smaller steps. He was all forward movement then, desperate to capture what he could of the city while he had the chance. Now he moves with more intention, with less urgency to prove and conquer and taste, as if the years have given him permission to take up space differently. Now he trusts that the world will come to him.

Eventually, we find an open bench around the perimeter of the fountain. I sit, and Reid sits beside me.

"I think this is pretty blissful." Reid rests his elbows on his knees.

"That guy is your bliss?" I cock a thumb toward a man in a rainbow knitted cap and a pair of beat-up Nikes who is standing on a literal soapbox, bellowing about ascending from the sins of the flesh in a divine spaceship.

"Who, the Heaven's Gate guy? I love that guy."

"It is very nineties. Fitting."

I don't have my camera with me, but this is too good not to document. I dig out my phone from my bag and take a picture of the man, who stands with his arms outstretched, as if conducting an invisible symphony, his mouth an open rictus. His posture brings to mind the weather-beaten statues of ancient Roman orators. But draped in his layers of mismatched fabrics, he looks as if he's somehow emerged not from the museum's galleries but from its lost and found.

I glance up at Reid and find that he's been watching me. "I like seeing what you see," he says.

"Well, there's a lot to see here." I put my phone back in my bag and turn my attention fully toward Reid. In the sunlight, the gold flecks in his eyes seem to glow, and now I notice in more detail the way that time has carved into the architecture of his face, sharpening and hollowing and sanding down. The change doesn't diminish him; it only makes him a more honest version of who he once was, when he was only potential.

"Does the city feel the same as it did back then?" I ask.

"It's a little slicker now. More commercialized, more polished. But I think, at its core, it still feels like a wildly fucked-up place to live." We both laugh. "I say that with respect. You know, working in entertainment . . . sometimes I wonder whether I'm becoming habituated to the facade of it all. Numbed to anything real." Reid gestures toward the fountain, overrun by screeching kids, darting in and out of the jets of water. “New York wears its heart on its sleeve. I like that about it.”

“I think it suits you.”

Reid pauses, his head tilted in thought. “I hope so. Or—I’ve always wanted it to. I work with smart, substantive people, and I’m proud of what I’ve made. But at the end of the day, LA is built on smoke and mirrors. I understand this—I am one of the guys making the smoke and hanging the mirrors—but sometimes I catch myself giving into the illusion. Believing that it’s concrete.” He sighs deeply. “I don’t know. With Gracie leaving soon, I’m starting to see that I’ve pinned everything, my entire identity, on being her dad and writing movies. But I’ve been in the Hollywood machine for so long—”

“And you won an Oscar.”

Reid laughs. “I did do that.” He glances at me. “Have you seen *Notting Hill*?”

“Surely that’s a rhetorical question.”

“So you’ll remember when Julia Roberts says that the men she dates go to sleep with the character she plays, and they wake up with the real person. That’s almost what it felt like to win. That night was . . . a circus. It was surreal. But I still had to get up the next morning, shave, make coffee, take my kid to school. Figure out what to work on next, what will actually make me happy, because expecting to reach that level of recognition a second time is fucking insanity. And even if I did . . . what would it mean, what would it change?” He runs a hand over his face, and I catch a glimpse of aggrieved exhaustion. "Anyway, I just happened to have a very nice decorative object on my bookshelf while I did those things."

"Ah. So that's where you keep it."

"A less creative choice than Kate Winslet. She keeps a few in her bathroom."

I put a hand on his arm, giving it a reassuring squeeze. I can't seem to help myself. "One day, you, too, will have so many Oscars that you'll have no choice but to put some above your toilet."

He knocks his knee into mine, letting it linger there for a few seconds. My body instinctively remembers the weight of his, the singular way we align together. I inch closer to him and catch another whiff of his skin—it's warm and musky, with the barest hint of white flowers. *This must be the hotel body wash*, I think, and then I'm assaulted with an image of him in the shower—

"I appreciate your belief in me," Reid says, bringing me back to our bench. "But I've made peace with the fact that I don't need that to happen again. In a lot of ways, the best thing that award did for me was free me up from the pressure to prove myself. Now I can just try to make good stuff. Whatever that means these days." He shrugs. "Besides, stepping on Cate Blanchett's train on the red carpet once was enough."

I inhale sharply. "You didn't."

"I sure did. She gave me this look like *I'm not angry, I'm just disappointed*." He shakes his head. "I will see that look on my deathbed."

I laugh. "That thing you were saying about compartmentalizing—I know how you feel. Since my divorce, I think I've kept my world pretty small. Funneling all my energy into Emme. Taking on projects that pay the bills but don't really challenge me creatively. Focusing on being high functioning. Protecting myself from pain but also any real shot at happiness."

"About that divorce." Reid picks a piece of lint off the knee of my pants. "I'm sensing there's a bigger story there."

Usually I would shrink away from answering, allowing myself all the excuses: It's boring. It hurts too much. It's in a past I deeply regret. But Reid was honest with me, and even with my parents, despite how hard it clearly was for him to share. The least I can do is return the trust. I *want* to do that for him. I take a deep breath.

"So, everything you need to know about James and me, you can probably learn from our wedding," I start. "It was this big, lavish affair that somehow snowballed from a city hall ceremony to a two-hundred-person blowout. James and I only danced together once, during our first dance—"

"What was the song?"

"Sade's 'By Your Side.'"

"Ironic."

"Oh, you don't even know. I barely saw him the rest of the evening."

He asks, *What could he have possibly been doing?* with his brows.

I shrug. "Schmoozing. I had to tug at his coattails to get his attention."

"Tails, huh?"

"It was Tavern on the Green in 1998."

"What'd you wear?"

When I eye him thoughtfully, curious about his interest in the minute details of one of my more haunted memories, he just shrugs. "I'm a visual learner," he explains.

Still, I choose to take this curiosity personally. "An ivory silk slip dress, cut on the bias. Buttons running down the back. We all wanted to be Carolyn Bessette back then." I sigh, remembering the way the fabric flowed over my hips like cool water. "That was the one decision I got to make."

I feel Reid's eyes skim over me. "I wish I'd seen you in that."

My skin heats underneath his gaze. "You can, actually. I kept the dress, chopped the train, and dyed it black. It was too beautiful to give away."

"You do look good in silk. I recall."

When I look at him again, he seems . . . bashful. An expression I may have seen on him as a twenty-two-year-old, but not as a full-blown adult. It's adorable.

"You recall me in silk?" My voice is so quiet, I wonder if I'll have to repeat myself.

"That dress is seared into my memory, Lili."

We're sitting close enough that I can see the steady pulse of his heartbeat in his neck. It would be so easy to move toward that spot—the spot that once felt like a safe harbor. It would be so easy to graze my lips over that spot, to capture that pulse in my mouth.

His gaze scans slowly across my face, and it's clear he's thinking about this too. He takes in a sharp breath.

But then he runs a hand down his face, clears his throat. "So the ex," he says.

"The who?"

He laughs. "Had he always been so distant with you? Or was that the first time you really noticed it?"

I try to bring myself back to my wedding day, to haul that moment from the depths of my memory.

"You know, I think it's the latter. James is . . . complicated. When he first meets people, he's warm and charismatic. He wants them to feel comfortable around him. That's how he made me feel, too, at the start. But that kind of attention drops off once he earns a person's trust. After the wedding, when we settled into our regular life, he just kept drifting away from me."

"Sounds lonely."

"It was. Initially I thought it was OK. Healthy, even. We each had our own things going on—he had his work, his routines, his goals, and I had mine. I'd always wanted to find freedom inside of a relationship, and I thought I'd found it in all that space between us."

"There's a difference between freedom and—well. Go on."

I nod. "A couple years into our marriage, I tried to confront him about the distance between us, suggested we could at least schedule regular time together. He made us a dinner reservation for the following week, then never again. It was always on me to beg for his time. Eventually it just became too depressing to keep asking. And for a while, I convinced myself that I was happy to trade his attention for the security our marriage provided. I convinced myself that that was enough." The anger roiling inside me breaks into a rich and profound sadness. "We lived like that for almost ten years."

Reid is quiet for a moment, like he's absorbing the story. He clenches his jaw, then unclenches it. "You deserve so much more than that."

I want people to be nice to you. I remember how Reid saying that simple phrase to me in Bryant Park five million years ago had made me feel worth protecting. It was different from my parents' protectiveness, which always had an anxious edge to it, like I was a fragile artifact encased in bubble wrap. Reid had made me feel precious, but not breakable.

Now Reid shakes his head and lets out a humorless laugh. "Sounds like he's a great doctor, but also an asshole."

"That about says it."

"So how did Emme fit into all this?" He looks at me apologetically.

"I know it seems misguided to bring a baby into this dynamic—believe me, I do. But I was hopeful that she would bring out all the best parts of him. In retrospect, it was incredibly naive."

He runs his hand back and forth across his jaw. "Is it naive? Or did you just hope to see the best in someone you loved?" There's a beat of silence, and I get the sense that he's gone somewhere I can't quite follow. Finally, he shakes his head. "You can't blame yourself for believing that."

I sigh. "I suppose so. Honestly, I think I wanted to have a child more than I wanted to fix my marriage. James just kept kicking the can down the road. First he had to finish his residency. Then his fellowship. Then pass the boards. Then adjust to his nighttime shifts. Then adjust back to his daytime shifts. And then I was thirty-four, and I knew that if I didn't insist on having a baby then, James would let another ten years go by. And when we had her . . . my marriage didn't get better. It didn't slow down James's pace. But my life started making sense again."

Reid smiles. "That's how I felt when we had Gracie. She was like this extra puzzle piece that I didn't even realize was missing."

"I know I hardly know her, but Gracie seems like an amazing girl, Reid. A little scary. But amazing."

Reid nods in agreement. "She gets the 'a little scary' thing from her mom. She was a force, and Gracie is too. But they both have these enormous hearts." Reid tilts his head. "It's taken a little extra work to keep her grounded, but between me, Cat, and my mom—"

"You've done great," I say.

Reid's use of present tense to describe his late wife isn't lost on me. I want to ask more about her, but I still feel uncomfortable prying. Like I'm stuck in this purgatory of both barely knowing Reid and having known him forever.

Then Reid looks at me, opens his mouth to say

something, and quickly closes it again. "I want to ask you something," he says, "but I don't want you to take it the wrong way."

"Just say it."

"I'll be less embarrassed if we're walking." He gets up from the bench and holds his hand out for me. I take it and stand. We drop palms, and I feel the loss in the marrow of my bones as we start winding around the park.

Finally, he says, "Why aren't you dating anyone?"

I can't help but laugh. "Why would you be embarrassed to ask me that?"

He appraises me for a moment. "Maybe not embarrassed. But I might be afraid to hear the answer."

"Well, I am a very intimidating person," I joke.

"You are, actually, very intimidating. Smart. Talented. Gorgeous."

I don't know how to respond to that. Reid just cocks his head at me, as if to say, *I speak the truth.*

I focus my eyes straight ahead of me. "I've gone on dates here and there since, but nothing serious. The dating pool gets exponentially smaller as you get older. Well, if you're a woman." Reid presses a hand to the small of my back to guide me around a skateboard abandoned in the middle of the pathway. His palm is warm and solid beneath the fabric of my shirt. "So there aren't a ton of options out there to begin with, and among the men I have met, I just haven't liked any of them enough to put in the work of a relationship. Honestly, though, the divorce offered a lot of relief, after the initial gut punch of it all. Trying to hold together a shoddily built marriage . . . it took a huge toll on me, in pretty much every conceivable way. Sometimes I feel like I'm still catching my breath."

"That makes sense," Reid says, but he seems to be turning something over in his mind.

"How about you?" I, too, am afraid to hear the answer, but once I ask, I realize I'd simply assumed that Reid was single. What if he's not?

"Same story. A few casual relationships, but nothing stuck." He says it casually, but from the slight tension that sneaks into his shoulders, I can tell this is a topic he's used to skirting. I recognize the response—I've done it myself.

"Really? What's wrong with you?" I joke.

Reid laughs. "Is working too much a good enough reason?"

"Sure," I say. "But I doubt it's the only one."

"I would venture to say we're both afraid of losing more than we already have."

How very Reid of him, to topple my carefully constructed facade with a simple, incisive comment.

"And yet, here we are." I spread my arms wide at the park. "With parents getting older, kids going to college."

"And at the end of the day, you're still standing there on your own, trying to hold all the pieces together."

Yes, and who *is* the person that I'm trying to hold together? Does Reid recognize her? Can he spot the girl I once was? It's been a while since someone held a mirror up, asked me to explain the choices that have brought me here. And now, peering in, I find myself in unfamiliar territory. I see her, this woman I've become, like viewing a painting from too close and then stepping back: the brushstrokes make sudden, startling sense. I understand the circumstances that shaped me, the small, accumulated moments that pressed me into this form.

But if twenty-year-old Lili were to materialize now, what would she think? Would she be disappointed? She believed that something good, maybe even radiant, was waiting for her once she had finally crossed to the other side of her fear. And yes, there have been times when I've stepped into the unknown, learned to tap into my own authority. I even survived a heartbreak that had, at moments, felt unsurvivable. In its wake, I constructed a life that makes me feel secure.

But what else? Now I worry that I've kept that *something more* at a distance—that the security itself is a trap I laid.

"Well," I say. "That got bleak."

"We've barely scratched the surface of bleak, baby."

I laugh, because I know this is true. I've offered him snippets of my heartbreak, but I can only imagine how deep his grief runs.

But I also know that, on this perfect June day—likely the only one we'll get—we need to lighten the mood. I think we've earned that.

"You know what we need?" I ask.

Reid arches an eyebrow at me. "I have an idea of what we need, but I'd like to hear what you have to say first."

His voice is warm honey, sticky with intention, and it

sends a rush of electricity through my body. I instinctively suck in air and swallow, which only intensifies the sensations of warmth gathering beneath my chest and between my legs. I bite my lip, trying to return to the moment.

"I was going to say more champagne." My throat is dry, my voice rasping.

"I'll take it," he says, his eyes catching the light.

We leave the park and pause at the corner of Waverly, our bodies reluctant to move. A bar would mean more noise, more bodies, more demands on our attention. And right now, I just want privacy. I just want Reid for myself.

I gesture up ahead, vaguely in the direction of my house. "I have a bottle at home, if you want to come over. I'm about thirty seconds that way."

I know what I'm asking, and I know he does too. *Come home with me. Close the door all the way.* The invitation floats between us, hovering there for a moment, caught in the morass of possibility. I wait for it to fall, or to be caught.

Reid's eyes glitter with mischief. "I think I can make it that long."

XI

We pause on the landing of my stoop as I dig around my bag for my keys. Behind me, I sense Reid's gaze sweep over me. I can't seem to get my hands to work. Or my eyes.

"You sure you want more alcohol?" Reid jokes.

"This is not an alcohol problem," I say. I tear open my bag and stick my face halfway into it, attempting to decode the shapeless mass of objects inside. "This is a reading-glasses problem. They seem to be the one object I didn't put in here."

Reid laughs, low in his chest. "Oh, there are glasses now? Hot."

I turn and raise an eyebrow at him. "Noted."

I finally find the keys and open the door. Reid follows me into the foyer, where I put my bag down on the vintage oak console. I sense him silently taking in the space: the celadon walls, the layered rugs in the living room, the black-and-white-checkered floors in the kitchen, and the antique, fluted green-glass chandelier hanging above us.

"This is a special place," he says. "It's very Lili."

"There's a lot of history here. And not all of it strictly mine. So I'll take that as a win."

I give him the CliffsNotes version of how I came to own this place: With immense foresight, my parents bought the Greek Revival townhouse in 1983, when it was worth about one-sixtieth of what it is now. They let it sit in its partially dilapidated state until fifteen years later, when they offered it to James and me as a wedding gift. We moved in and fixed it up.

Over the past twenty years, I've been nudged to sell by plenty of piratical realtors, but I'm never going to do it. This is where I created my first home, even if that was with James. This is where we brought Emme home from the hospital, where we experienced all her firsts together. And after James moved out, this is where Emme and I made another home together, just the two of us. This is my family's legacy.

Now I lead Reid toward the back of the house into the kitchen, which looks out onto the small garden. I'm proud of this place, but with Reid here, I can't help but notice all the things I keep meaning to take care of and putting off—weeding, finally Googling how to remove the stain Emme's blue nail polish left on the marble counter a year ago. I wonder what Reid's house looks like; I can't imagine it isn't orderly and calm, like him.

He grabs a stool at the island while I pull out a bottle of champagne from the fridge. It's probably too expensive for the occasion, left over from the small New Year's Eve party I hosted months ago, but if not now, when?

There's a catalog for an outdoor clothing company

sitting on the counter. Reid drags it toward him and starts absentmindedly flipping through it.

"Flute or coupe?" I move to the cabinet above the sink.

"Either." In the catalog, Reid points at a complicated-looking jacket with about ten thousand pockets and a utility belt hanging off the hem. "You'd look good in this."

"Reading glasses and performance wear, huh? I see your tastes have evolved."

"My taste is for the woman wearing the reading glasses and performance wear."

Our gazes lock. A current hums between us, low and steady, but ready to crest with the barest friction. His eyes are darker now, looking at me like I'm something he's been thinking about for days. Years.

My body responds before my mind can intervene—a buzz in my chest that flutters down to my hands. They itch to feel the fine layer of stubble on his jaw, the softness of his hair.

I should say something to acknowledge this frisson between us.

Instead, I break eye contact and turn toward the sink, busying myself with rinsing out the flute glasses, which have collected a shimmer of dust. The water runs too hot, but I don't adjust it, letting the sting of it ground me back into my body, tug me away from the fantasy.

Still, I feel him watching, his gaze landing between my shoulder blades.

"I don't know how this place got my address, but they've

been shaming me with these catalogs for years." I force my voice into an even tenor and turn back to the island, drying off the glasses. "I've never gone camping in my life."

Reid looks at me in mock horror. "Never? Not even a cabin in the woods?"

"That sounds like my personal nightmare."

"I hate to add to the shaming, but I think you're missing out. The quiet, the calm . . . it's really special. I started taking Gracie out to Big Bear from the time she was three. By six, she was catching fish and starting fires herself."

I let that sit for a minute, waiting for him to go on. I notice that he said *I*, not *we*. I know I won't be able to focus until he shares the rest of this story.

"Just the two of you?"

He nods. "Just us."

Reid flips through the catalog while I pour the wine, wondering how best to broach this subject. But then I'm just as quickly distracted by the way he concentrates on each page, how his eyes scan each word, a hand pressed over his mouth. How he offers even the most inconsequential things the dignity of his attention.

"Lili," he says casually, his gaze still fixed on a high-end portable fire pit. "I can hear you thinking."

I slide a glass toward him, then take a sip from my own, the bubbles bursting in my mouth. I lean against the island.

"I'm sorry," I say. "I don't mean to pry. I know this was supposed to be our having-fun time."

"Yeah. I can see how the dead wife gets in the way of

that." He says it jokingly, but I can still hear the strain in his voice.

"It can't be easy to share that with people you barely know. Or maybe—maybe sometimes it's easier to share with someone you barely know."

Reid nods, then looks out the sliding glass doors to the backyard. "It'll be ten years in September. Gracie was seven."

When he turns back to me, I see a slackness in his face, a dullness in his eyes. It doesn't look right on him. I want to put him back the way he was.

He tilts his flute toward me. "Might need something stronger than this."

I hold up a finger and duck into the locked butler's pantry, where I stashed all the hard alcohol once Emme started middle school. I come back with a bottle of whiskey and pull out two coffee mugs from our prolific collection of flea market finds: "I'm Too Sexy for 40," reads one with a *Sex and the City*–era black-and-pink color theme; the other is a classic diner mug, half an inch thick with a proud blue stripe running around the rim.

I pour a healthy glug into each and slide him the sexy mug. He looks at it and raises an eyebrow at me.

"It's true," I say, innocently.

"You think it's true now, you should've seen me when I was actually forty."

I gesture toward the mug. "Better?"

He takes a sip and nods. "That's good shit."

"Got me through my divorce."

I watch him readjust in the stool. He has another sip, bolstering himself, and takes a breath. Exhales. "Thea was one of the most charismatic people I have ever known. When she walked into a room, the energy shifted. I never understood what people meant when they talked about 'star quality' until I met her."

"Where did you two meet?"

"On a movie. A little indie my writing partner and I did in 2003. Our main character was an escort who witnesses an accidental homicide. This was at a time when sex workers were portrayed pretty one-dimensionally in movies, so we had our work cut out for us. We were confident in where our writing ended up, but I honestly wasn't sure we had the budget to get an actor who could play her the right way. But when I watched Thea on set, I just . . . I couldn't believe what I was seeing. She was magic. She completely disappeared into the part. And when she reemerged, she was still so *luminous*." He shakes his head. "I don't know. You'd think I'd be able to describe her better after knowing her for so many years, but I just always struggle to do her justice."

I nod, maybe too emphatically. Not being able to describe people with words—it's why I take photos.

"And I loved her, I really did. But I also loved that she loved me, you know? I loved that this otherworldly person somehow thought that I was important enough to be loved."

I'm distracted by the idea that Reid—*Reid*—would

ever think himself unworthy of love. But I nod. "I think I understand that."

"Yeah?" Reid looks up at me from underneath a heavy brow, his voice hoarse. Seeking validation. To know that he's not alone.

"I promise I'll stop talking about him, but it's a bit how I felt about James. When I met him, I was twenty-three, directionless, still living with Nisha in Alphabet City. And here was this twenty-eight-year-old doctor, clean-shaven and well-dressed. He thought my lifestyle was romantic and interesting, even though the bohemian thing was entirely unintentional. He made me feel like I was worth something, and I thought that maybe, with his influence, I could get myself together—be worthy of him."

"Funny," he says. "We both married people we thought we didn't deserve."

"*Funny* is one word," I say.

Reid clears his throat. "Thea had a troubled childhood, was in and out of rehab throughout her teens and into her early twenties. She'd been in recovery for almost five years when I met her, but I think our relationship gave her an extra boost of stability she could never quite find on her own. For the first few years of our relationship, she was holding down jobs, maintaining her friendships, taking good care of her health. But when we had Gracie . . . it's like we tripped a wire. She started using again soon after Gracie was born. When Gracie was three, Cat and I got Thea to go back into rehab, found her a therapist she liked.

She was working the program again. She was good again, for a while."

Reid looks out the window, like he's lost to the memory.

"And then one day, I get a call from the LAPD. I knew what they were going to say before I even picked up the phone." He runs a hand over his face, then drinks deeply from his coffee mug. When he speaks again, his voice is thick with emotion. "She ran off the road on Mulholland Drive. No one else was hurt, thank god, but they found enough ketamine in her system to kill a horse. When the police told me what happened, I laughed. It was the most deranged reaction, but I couldn't help it. Of course, my actress wife went out like she was in a fucking David Lynch movie."

"Did you know she was using again?" I bury my question in my own mug.

"At the time, I would have sworn I didn't. But when I look back on it, I remember moments when she would leave Gracie with me and disappear for a few hours. Or her behavior would be slightly off. She would get this glassy look in her eyes. Her reflexes were slow." He shakes his head. "I was so wrapped up in my work at that time. I'd just sold my first script to a major studio. I'd finally made enough money to put a down payment on a house for my mom. I was able to send Gracie to a private elementary school. I just loved my life. I was proud of what I had built. And I loved the idea of Thea being healthy so much that I couldn't see the reality through the fantasy." Reid laughs mirthlessly. "I've done a lot that I regret, but I will never forgive myself for letting my daughter grow up without her mom." His jaw tenses. "It was my job to protect them both, and I failed at it, spectacularly."

When he meets my gaze, the pain in his eyes is palpable. There's a particular texture to the hurt—not the raw bleed of a fresh wound, but calcified, like a foreign object his body has hardened around. And I can see how the story he's told himself of Thea's death—the liability he's assumed for it—has only pushed that object in deeper.

"Reid. You know you aren't responsible for Thea's death, right?"

"I would like to believe that's true. I know Gracie doesn't blame me for it."

"I *knew* I liked Gracie."

Reid laughs, and this time, there's a crack in the shell, a whisper of light seeping through. "I try to talk to Gracie about Thea as much as I can, to try to keep her alive. But she doesn't always want to engage. I think that's one of the reasons she wants to move out here for college. She wants a fresh start."

"I understand why you want to keep her close."

"Gracie is vigilant about avoiding drugs and alcohol, and she's been in therapy ever since her mom died. She's solid. I have every reason to trust her." Reid looks at me with such sincerity then, as if he's casting about for a buoy. I reach out and take his hand, to try to be that anchor for him. "But I can't help but worry . . . what if things take a turn for her, and I'm not there to see it?"

My heart breaks for them both. The unthinkable tragedy.

"You brought Gracie to New York. You let her see NYU and imagine what her life might be like here. You wouldn't do that unless you believed she could do it."

When he meets my eyes again, I can see the light there, the warmth, pushing against the edges of the darkness. "You're right. And also—I was glad to have an excuse to come to the show."

I sense that he had the same ridiculously far-fetched dream that I did: That magic would strike twice. Like the dream of an actual twenty-year-old.

We're both quiet for a moment, letting the enormity of what he just admitted settle over us.

Then Reid pulls my hand up to meet his mouth, pressing a kiss there, and that current of electricity sparks back up again, jolting my entire system awake. I'm suddenly aware that I've leaned almost entirely across the kitchen island to be closer to him—to the scent that once left me dazed and sated, that I loved so much, I would press my face into his T-shirts when he left for work.

And it fully dawns on me that our time together is limited. Again. I don't know if Reid wants anything more from me than this moment. I do know that embarking on anything more would require so much dexterity, so much grace. So much courage, on both our parts.

Maybe this is our curse: We come together, we fall apart. The last time I was with Reid, I made a pact with myself to be brave, to allow myself to be fully seen by him. I'm faced with the same choice yet again, but this time with a heart that's been bruised—by James, yes. But by Reid too.

Now every self-preserving instinct is screaming at me to step away. To go back to the calm, predictable environment I've constructed that keeps me safe. To make sure I don't break again.

And those same alarm bells are warning me not to risk mishandling Reid's shattered heart either.

But when his hand moves to trace my jaw, all those fears suddenly dissipate, and desire floods in. I know we're doomed, I know this is going nowhere, I know my heart will probably get stomped on again, but right now, I can't help myself.

I always needed more of him. And I still do.

XII

I round the island and come to stand in front of Reid. With him on the stool, we're about eye level. I cradle the sides of his face in both my hands. I feel my body sigh in relief, finally making contact with his skin. His eyes flutter closed as he tilts his head to rest in my palms.

"I like this." I run my fingers through the silver in his hair. "I like the gray."

"If you like the gray, I like the gray," he murmurs.

"We should check on the girls," I say, trusting that he understands the secret second meaning in my words—we need to know how much time we have right now.

"Gracie texted me on our way over here." His hand glides across my hip, and I lean into his warmth. "They're heading to Chinatown. Dim sum. I think."

We consider each other for half a second, and in that window, it's like we come to a silent, mutual agreement: Don't waste the time we've been given.

And when his arms circle my waist, when our lips scramble to meet in an insistent, deepening kiss, when his hands grab at the hem of my top and pull it up over my head, I am right back to the way I was magnetized to him in the basement of the bookstore so many years ago, how some unspoken law dictated we come together. I am stunned by the familiarity of the way he tastes and the feel of his mouth against mine—that my sense memory reaches back over so many decades feels like a drunken form of déjà vu.

He hooks an arm around my back, spreads his fingers wide, and comes to a stand, levering me off the ground on his way to his full height. I lean my chest into his and wrap my legs around his waist. My desire spirals, and I begin to move rhythmically against him, desperate for the friction of his belt buckle, the muscles straining beneath his shirt. I feel him hard underneath me and instinctively slide my hand to his crotch. Our mouths still locked together, tongues pushing greedily into each other, he backs us into the living room and lays me down on the couch.

He stands over me for a moment, his eyes glazed as he surveys me, like he's gathering himself before he begins some methodical, satisfying work. There's no trace of the heaviness I'd seen in him just a few minutes ago, and I take in, bask in, his reprieve.

He gazes at me expectantly, and I realize—he's waiting for my permission.

I run my fingers underneath the hem of his T-shirt. "Take this off."

He makes a quiet, pleased sound of approval. In a single movement, he reaches both hands behind his back and pulls the shirt over his head, leaving his hair unkempt.

I lift myself to sitting so that I'm eye level with his belt buckle. Slowly, deliberately, I unlatch it, delighting in the sound of the hardware coming undone, then even more in the noise Reid makes low in his throat, somewhere between a growl and a sigh. He runs a finger under my chin, lifting it so that our eyes meet.

I'm momentarily self-conscious about the way I might look to him. I'm happy in my body, but I'm not delusional: This is not the same body I had when I was nineteen. I wouldn't *want* it to be. But—

"Lili," he says softly. The way Reid says my name, a spell as always—it immediately puts to rest whatever is going on in my head. Time breaks, and I exist only inside the sound of his voice. I would let him do anything he wanted to me as long as he asked in that voice. "You're so fucking hot."

I touch a palm to his chest and press the pads of my fingers there.

Then we both turn impatient. His hands push through my hair, and my fingers shake as I unbutton his jeans and tear down his fly, as I run my thumb down his thickening cock. My mouth floods, ready to have him, and I shift onto one heel to press into the pulse building between my legs.

"*Fuck*," Reid says, as I trace my tongue down his stomach, slide my fingers inside his waistband, then push his briefs down just enough to free his length.

Before I can get any further, he drops down to his knees, maintaining a gentle hold on the back of my head, like he doesn't want to let me go. I can't read the look on his face as he pulls me in for a kiss. It's softer this time, lingering.

"Am I going too fast?" I ask when we pull apart.

Something inside me threatens to shutter. I worry I might be taking advantage of his vulnerability. Of mine. I sense I shouldn't have abandoned my instincts like I did, should have maintained my self-control.

But he just laughs, then runs his thumb between my brows. "No," he shakes his head. When he reaches down to undo the button of my jeans and release my zipper with maddening control, whatever fears I had melt away again.

His mouth runs across my cheek, over to my ear. "I just needed to get to you, before you got to me."

He leans me back, tugs my jeans over my knees, and kisses across my stomach, along my thighs. Then he dips two fingers in his mouth and slides his hand down my stomach, into my underwear, between my legs. His breath turns heavy as he runs those fingers along my seam. It feels so *young* to have his hands on me like this, on my couch with my pants half on. My knees open wider for him, my hips lifting to meet him, to coax him into me.

"You feel so fucking good," he says, more to himself than to me, as he dips inside me and begins to move with the cadence of my hips, his thumb teasing my clit in steady circles. I feel my senses rearrange around that single point of contact, and I have never needed anything more than I need this: Reid's head buried in my neck, his strength contained and focused on me, his satisfied moans that echo my own.

"Reid," I plead. I tighten my hold around his neck, seeking an anchor as his fingers find that spot against my front wall and my vision blurs and splinters.

"I got you," he whispers back, and I think—I know—that I have never felt this way before, on the edge of finding a relief I didn't know could be mine. I'm getting agonizingly closer with every stroke, and that's exactly when we both hear it: two voices at the front door.

Two voices we would know anywhere.

We both stop abruptly, frozen in fear, our eyes locked in part panic, part disbelief, willing time to do us a solid and slow down again, the way it did earlier.

And when it doesn't—when the voices grow closer, interrupted by the jangle of keys, then the slide of a key in the lock—we simultaneously move into action. Reid launches himself off me, buckles his belt, helps me back into my shirt, and bounds into the kitchen, where I hear him washing his hands—a smart touch—and putting our champagne and whiskey glasses in the sink before coming back into the living room and handing me a glass of water. I smooth my hair, wipe a smear of lip balm from my chin, and take a seat beside Reid on the couch, keeping an appropriate amount of distance between us.

Before the girls enter the foyer, all screeching laughs and tinkling purse charms, we have just enough time to trade a warily victorious look. And then he risks it all by reaching out to tuck a lock of hair behind my ear, as if he can't help himself. I understand the impulse: It requires everything in me not to take that hand and press it to my mouth.

"Hi guys," I say, my voice chipper. "We thought you were going to Chinatown?"

Emme startles, pressing a hand against her chest—the same thing my mother just did at lunch. Eerie.

"Shit." She drops an armful of shopping bags on the floor. "Sorry, I mean, *wow*. We wanted to come back and hang for a second. I thought you guys would still be at lunch."

She seems surprised, but not onto us. Gracie, however, does not seem to be so easily convinced. She saunters into the living room behind Emme, arms crossed over her chest. I watch her survey the scene coolly, her face impassive as she takes in me, then Reid, then the rest of the room: the water sloshed over the glasses on the coffee table, the striped red pillow that must have fallen to the floor at some point.

Shit.

"Their reservation was, like, five hours ago," Gracie says, her eyes still trained on that damning pillow. "It would be crazy if they were still at the restaurant."

Then Gracie redirects her attention to me. She gives me a smirk, but it's not unkind. It's very possible that I'm still drunk on endorphins, but I think the look on her face is . . . subtly amused? She clearly knows that something went on here, and a glance at Reid's hair, uncharacteristically mussed, confirms that we did not do as good a job with the cleanup as we'd hoped.

Is it possible that Gracie *approves* of me?

Then my daughter, adorably oblivious to what's going on here, plops down on the armchair across from Reid and me. "Maybe they did a bop," she trills. "It's a beautiful day for a bop."

"We went to Nana and Papa's—I texted you earlier," I say to the one teenager in the world who never looks at her phone. "Then we did do a bop, around the park."

Gracie squeezes in beside Emme, and Emme slings an arm over her leg with the casual affection of teenage girls. I'm a little surprised by how quickly they've bonded after the nightmare of their first encounter.

"Speaking of five hours"—Reid looks at his watch, no longer a scuffed Timex—"Grace, you and I should head back uptown if you want to change before Dirt Candy. Reservation's at seven."

Emme and Gracie exchange a look so subtle, I'm sure Reid didn't clock it.

But I did.

"No!" Emme says quickly, grabbing on to Gracie's arm with both her hands. "Don't leave. Why don't you guys stay for dinner? Mom and I were going to cook."

I don't remember any such plans, but I'll go along with it if it keeps Reid here. I catch a glimpse of his fingers around the glass, and I am suddenly, ridiculously wistful for just a few minutes earlier. As much as I want to finish what we started, I also don't want to be left to process what just happened on my own.

More than that, it just feels *right* for him to stay. And Gracie too.

"I just did a big grocery run," I say, playing along. "Gracie, I can make a veggie chili, if that sounds good. I think we have some dairy-free cheddar in the fridge."

"It melts just like real cheese!" Emme adds.

I glance over at Reid, who seems genuinely in the dark about whatever conspiracy the girls are scheming about. The man may be smart, but he's never been a teenage girl.

"That is, if your dad's OK with it," I add. "I don't want to make you miss the restaurant."

"Sounds great to me," Reid says. "Gracie?"

"Yeah, I'm getting sick of restaurant food." Gracie unfurls herself from the chair, stretches her arms above her head, and makes her way into the kitchen, where I hear cabinets begin to bang open and shut.

I bite back a smile as Emme follows, leaving Reid and me on the couch. Reid runs a hand through his hair and gives me that upside-down smirk. I have to tense my muscles, force my body to stay where I am, not to climb into his lap and rub myself against him like a cat.

"You're sure this is OK?" I ask. "I don't want to impose."

Reid laughs, quietly enough for the girls not to hear. "Lil," he says into my ear, "you are never going to be an imposition." The tickle of his warm breath sends a tingle down my neck.

Then he gives me a quick kiss at the corner of my mouth, stands, and holds his hand out to help me up.

XIII

The four of us manage the delicate dance of working together in the kitchen, a potentially disastrous endeavor. This mostly involves Reid and me actually making the food, while the girls perch on the stools and monitor the playlist and sip peach-flavored sparkling water. We cobble together some kind of pantry-dump chili garnished with tortilla chips, plus a green salad mostly made of herbs. Reid makes guacamole. "The secret is in not putting a bunch of unnecessary shit in it," he says. "Just the avocados, a little bit of sweet onion, salt, and lime juice."

Watching Reid confidently move between the stove and a cutting board triggers the memory of cooking together in my East Village apartment. It was less a kitchen proper than it was a row of semibroken appliances, but it felt more substantial with Reid maneuvering in it.

Him here, now, unlocks a whole new genre of competence porn. My mouth literally waters as I watch him peel and dice an onion, neatly pile the uniform cubes onto the edge of a big butcher's knife, and slide them into the pot with one finger.

When the food is almost ready, the girls set the table,

complete with cloth napkins, which Emme and I never bother with when it's just the two of us. Then Emme switches off the overheads, turns on the collection of table lamps scattered around the room—our one rule in the house: no big lights after 5 p.m.—and brings a few taper candles to the table. Gracie produces a sterling-silver lighter that looks like a piece of heavy jewelry from the doll-sized pocket of her low-rise jeans and ignites them.

We sit at the table just as the sun sets. The kitchen floods with rose-gold light. The girls tell us about stumbling upon the anarchist book fair at Judson Memorial Church, where a grandmotherly type in a homemade crocheted vest extolled the virtues of community structured around mutual aid. Emme shares how the woman had stitched each minuscule yellow petal of each of the countless daffodils adorning her vest. Gracie opines about the differences between old New York hippies and old LA hippies. And I watch Reid. I love the way he regards his daughter when she speaks, with genuine interest and care, and that he offers the same respect to Emme.

I know something dangerous is happening here: We're playing house. It's seductively easy to imagine doing this every night, to all come together at the end of the day and commiserate around the kitchen table.

I know this delusion is a symptom of my almost-orgasm-addled brain, and it's ridiculous to entertain it. But I also can't deny how good it feels to allow myself to want more. To thrust myself into this moment, unburdened by reality.

As Emme shows us the sunflower pins the woman

doled out after her lecture (*Action, Freedom, Unity*, they read), my phone rings from where I left it, face down on the island. When I step away and see it's James calling, all the goodwill I'd just cultivated vanishes, a swollen balloon popped with a scalpel.

I excuse myself to take the call in my bedroom, and as I turn toward the stairs, I see that Emme's expression has melted in worry, like she already knows what's coming.

Protective anger grows inside me, flushing my face with blood.

"Hi," I say briskly when I answer and close my door. "What is it?"

As Emme would say, today I'm choosing violence.

James breathes a laugh like steam. "Hello to you too. How's your evening going?" In the background, I hear the muffled machine beeps and efficient murmurs of the hospital.

"I have guests over, so I don't really have time to talk," I say. "What's going on?"

"OK, then." The rustle of papers, a whispered aside to someone passing behind him. "So, listen, I know Emme and I have been trying to make this Broadway thing work, but—"

"Actually, Emme *has* been making it work. She's rearranged her schedule and adjusted her expectations twice now. You're the one who hasn't been able to figure your shit out."

When we first got divorced, we made an agreement that if James's schedule changed, he would communicate that through me. Not Emme. I am her primary caretaker, and the onus should be on me to bear the burden of her father's volatility.

So I'd always thought.

But now that she's fifteen, and I've left her downstairs with that look in her eyes, I'm beginning to think that this arrangement is unfair to all three of us. I don't want Emme to have to navigate these conversations with her father, but I wonder if I'm doing a disservice to her maturity by depriving her of the opportunity to do that.

And why should I continue to be the bearer of James's bad news? If *he* was the one to hear the hurt in Emme's voice, to see the disappointment on her face, would he be so quick to let her down? By trying to protect Emme, have I just made it easier for James to hurt her?

"So I know we have tickets to tomorrow night, but unfortunately I'm going to have to—"

I sit down on the bed and hold the phone away from my ear while James goes on. If I have to hear every word, I will break a fragile object. Instead, I let his speech mix with fragments of what's happening downstairs: Emme's laugh, Gracie groaning at some invisible offense, the playlist ramping up from a soft country mix to bossa nova. And anchoring everything, Reid's deep, steady voice.

Now I put the phone back to my ear.

"I really don't need to hear whatever complex excuse it is," I say.

"Don't be ridiculous, Lil. You know what my work is like."

I pinch the bridge of my nose and bring my voice down an octave. I want him to receive what I'm saying, not dismiss it as an overemotional rant. Which, I can admit, I've been known to dole out. "I know you have lives to save, and you know I respect you for it. But at this point, you are consciously choosing your work over your daughter." I take a breath, shoring myself up to say what I should have told him years ago. "And I won't cover for you anymore. From here on out, you need to call her directly if you change your plans. I can't keep being the middleman."

"I am sorry, Lil." When James speaks, I can hear the pain in his voice. So he heard me. A Pyrrhic victory, I suppose. "And I'm sorry to put you in this position. You know I get caught up in this . . . intensity."

"I do know that," I say. "But our time with Emme is . . ."

"Dwindling? I know that too. Last time she was with me, she told me she wanted to look at Bennington. Like, bumfuck-Vermont Bennington. Four-hour-drive-away Bennington."

"She told me that too. She's in a Donna Tartt phase."

James laughs. "Explains why she asked to borrow one of my ties."

"It pains me to admit it, but I do think she could be happy at a smaller school, outside the city. Apparently Bennington has a student-run farm she's interested in working on."

"Yeah, but Vermont? Sarah Lawrence is a small school. It has grass. And it's, what, a thirty-minute train ride away?

I don't like the idea of her driving alone for hours. She doesn't even have her license."

"Of course she doesn't have her license! She hasn't even started driver's ed." I laugh through a sigh as I process what James and I are doing right now: Talking about our kid like two concerned parents. "You know, it's sweet that you want her close. I think she'd appreciate hearing that from you."

"Yeah," he says. He takes a deep, jagged breath. "Unfortunately, about tomorrow, I really have overextended myself, and I don't see a way to back out of it. But Emme and I can do something fun this weekend, when I have her. Whatever she wants."

"You'll call her and tell her that yourself."

"I will."

"And we're using those *& Juliet* tickets for tomorrow."

"As you should."

We hang up, and I head back downstairs, where Reid, Gracie, and Emme have started a game of Uno at the table, their bowls pushed to the side. When I come in, Reid's concerned eyes lift to meet mine, and he puts his cards down.

I sit next to Emme, who pulls her knees to her chest. "Was that Dad?"

I pour the last of the wine into my glass. "It was Dad."

"He's canceling again," she says.

I try to put my hand on her back, but she wriggles away. "I'm sorry, sweetie. He's going to call you later and talk about it. But you and I can still go to the show tomorrow, if you're up for it."

"Mm-hmm." Emme picks up her spoon and looks down into her bowl, pushing the remnants of her chili around in a swirling pattern. I always think she looks like a baby at this angle, all cheek and lash. I wish I could gather her up in my arms. I would, if she didn't clearly want some space, if I wasn't afraid of embarrassing her in front of Gracie.

From across the table, I catch Reid sink back in his chair and cross his arms over his chest like he's holding something in. I lift my shoulders at him: *This is how it goes.* To which he tilts his head and huffs a laugh under his breath: *Jerk.*

"Which show were you planning to see?" Reid directs this question at Emme, but she gives no indication of responding. She's stewing, separating the corn kernels from the kidney beans inside her bowl.

"*& Juliet*," I say.

"Supposed to be great, I hear." Reid glances over at Gracie. Her cards are still fanned, and she's observing this exchange like a tennis match. "Why don't Gracie and I see if we can get tickets, tag along? I haven't taken her to a Broadway show yet. It's a gross oversight in her New York education."

"Musicals make me want to die," Gracie responds. Reid shoots her a look. She puts her cards down and sighs. "But I am here to collect new experiences, so I would be willing to sacrifice myself. For the plot."

I like this idea—of course I like this idea—and I know Reid has the best intentions in proposing it. But I'm not confident that Emme will feel the same. She tries to take her disappointment in stride, but from the way she's shutting down, I know she's struggling to bounce back.

And even if she says she likes him, Reid is not going to take the edge off her dad bailing on her.

"Em?" I ask her as gently as I can, not wanting my own feelings to interfere.

Emme drops her spoon in her bowl. "I don't know. I don't think I want to go anymore."

When she finally looks at me, there's a pleading in her eyes—she wants me to take her out of this situation. I've pushed her too far.

"That's OK," I say. Then, to Reid, "We'll let you and Gracie have your time together tomorrow. We've taken up way too much of it already."

His single parent's sixth sense activated, Reid nods, then looks at his watch and reminds Gracie that they're getting up early tomorrow to hit the Met when it opens, before the crowds flood in.

The mood is notably subdued as we clean up, but Emme, allergic to dead air, makes a heroic effort at small talk.

Before they leave, Emme shows Gracie to the bathroom, leaving Reid and me alone in the kitchen. I head over to the sink to soak the soup pot. He comes up behind me and pulls my hair over one shoulder, grazing a light kiss over my neck.

"I think I pushed a boundary there," he says. "I'm sorry."

The sensation of him behind me, the insistence of his touch, the gentleness with which he handles me . . . it's suddenly too overwhelming, heightening the warring desires within me. I want him, but I worry that the wanting threatens the fragile equilibrium I've established for my life, for Emme's.

I step to the side, subtly extricating myself from his hold, though it pains me to leave his orbit. Gracefully, he takes another step in the other direction, creating more space between us.

"Don't worry about it," I say. "This stuff with her dad . . . it's complicated. For me and for her. She puts him on a pedestal, but then he turns around and does things like this. It's hard for her to square who he is in her head with who he is." I shake my head, becoming more and more agitated. "I've been trying to protect Emme, but I'm worried that it's done more harm than good. I don't want her to be delusional about people, believing the best in everyone, then being burned when they show their true colors."

Reid is quiet for a beat. "I'm really trying not to have opinions about your ex right now."

There's something . . . not quite distant in his voice, but hard. Assertive. Clearly, he's been sitting on these feelings, calculating whether to share them or keep stewing.

"But you do," I say.

"Of course I do. The guy consistently disappoints his kid, and you're the one who has to clean up the mess." He shakes his head, then leans against the island, closer to me. "I'm sorry. I might be overstepping here. Again. I just . . . our girls have been through some tough stuff."

I feel my stress levels ratcheting up in response to the

way he says this, so plainly, the pressure valve in me threatening to break. And then it does, before I can recalibrate it. "Reid, I can't do this. Play house with you." It comes out angrier than I'd expected. "We're the parents, and this kind of thing—we're making their lives harder." As soon as the words escape my mouth, I wish I could stuff them back in. I hadn't meant for them to sound like an assault on Reid's own judgments. But from the way his expression collapses and his arms fold protectively over his chest, I know he feels the sting.

"I'm sorry," I say, scrambling to salvage what I can. "That came out worse than I meant it. I just meant . . ."

"No, Lil. I think you meant exactly what you said." Reid's voice is quiet now, but there's steel underneath it. He straightens, putting more distance between us. "Maybe it's for the best that things aren't going to work out tomorrow."

The tenderness from moments before has evaporated, replaced by something raw, edged with hurt.

"OK," I manage, my heart collapsing in on itself. "But . . . I do want to see you again. Both of you. If you want to."

Reid's eyes find mine again, and I notice the barest flicker of something in them—wistfulness, maybe, or at least the possibility of it.

"Do you?" Reid's tone is even, like there is no wrong answer. "I need you to be honest with me here. Not careful, not protective—just honest."

I realize how unfamiliar this is. With James, I was never punished for obfuscation and rewarded for honesty. I was just . . . left alone. Now Reid's challenge hangs in the air, waiting for me to take it and run—or to back down from it.

"I want to see you again," I say. The words feel insufficient. But they're real.

Reid studies my face for a long moment, and I can see him taking in my statement, weighing whether it's enough to surmount what just happened here. Before he has a chance to respond, Emme and Gracie come bustling back into the kitchen, their laughter breaking up the tension that just hung between us.

We all move toward the foyer, and Emme gives Gracie a hug goodbye, then surprises me by offering one to Reid too.

Then Reid turns to me, hesitating, and the pause that follows splits the air like a current. In that pause, I imagine that his arms might circle me, his mouth might find mine, and all his hurt might be erased, and so might mine. And in that fantasy, I'd be done for, absolutely done for; my bones turned to stardust, gathering in that perfect spot between his neck and his collarbone, where his skin smells like yesterday and tomorrow.

But Reid doesn't do that. He can't. Instead, he grazes a hand down my arm, too quickly for the girls to conceive of it as anything of consequence. He says something about tomorrow, tossed like a promise he wishes he could keep, but the truth is that I don't know if I'll see him again. I refuse to feel guilty about that—for prioritizing self-preservation, and for keeping Emme safe—but I can't ignore the sadness that shrouds me as I close the door behind them.

XIV

I wake up early the next morning and spend the next four hours in the kind of fugue state that only focused work can offer. I was supposed to deliver photos from the tribute show yesterday, so now I'm in overdrive, uploading, sorting, and editing. With the images blown up on my desktop, each face in the crowd is magnified, every grain and highlight thrown into clearer relief. I can't help but look for Reid. I don't find him anywhere.

I'm done by ten, around when Emme ambles down to the kitchen in a worn-out Pixies T-shirt that drops down to her knees, a hand-me-down from her dad.

I glance at the oven clock. *Reid and Gracie should be getting to the Met*, I think.

The way we left things last night, I know that I need to be the one to reach out to him. It was *my* temper—my fear—that flared in an act of . . . I'm not sure what. Last night I would have said I was safeguarding something sacred, but why do I feel singed? And why do I keep staring at my phone dumbly, as if a text from Reid will materialize out of thin air? Why am I so scared to act on what I want, now that it's within reach?

I leave my phone on the kitchen table and put on a pot of water for tea. I won't let Emme have coffee yet, but she likes the ritual of drinking something hot in the morning.

Emme opens the French doors leading out to the garden, then settles into the stool across from me. I slide over her cup, heavy with honey. Distantly, I hear the telescopic whine of a siren, the staccato sparkle of birdsong.

She takes a sip. "I talked to Dad this morning. He called me."

I raise my eyebrows. It's probably not fair of me to be surprised that James actually stuck to our plan, but I can't help myself.

"Oh yeah?"

"He apologized for not being able to take me to the show. One of the other attendings fell off his motorcycle and is out of commission for a few weeks, so he has to cover for him. He understands that this is a profoundly unfair reason, but apparently the entire hospital system would crumble without him there." She rolls her eyes into her tea. "You know, he's kind of an asshole. Not to me, exactly, but like . . . in general."

Which makes me feel like I've been stabbed in the gut with a thousand tiny needles. But this is what I wanted, isn't it? For Emme to finally have a clear-eyed understanding of her father?

"Your dad's not perfect—none of us are—but he's not a bad person," I say. I think it might be true.

"I'm starting to get why he was hard to be married to."

I pause, trying to craft a diplomatic response.

"I knew your dad had to put his whole self into his patients to be the best surgeon he could. That's what I signed up for when I married him—it's something I admired about him. But you're right, it wasn't easy to be chosen second. It did make me feel lonely."

But you know this, I think. My heart wrings inside my chest. *He does the same thing to you.*

She stirs her tea bag around in her smiley-face mug. "Do you think Reid would be easy to be married to?"

I let out a shocked laugh. This girl has never not kept me on my toes. "I'm not sure," I say, acting like I've never considered it.

"Gracie wants him to get married again, because she's worried about what'll happen to him when she goes to college. She thinks he uses her and his work as a way to escape, and when she's gone, he'll only have that one thing, which is unwise, considering how erratic his business is. Grace says even an Oscar isn't enough to guarantee your long-term success. And what would he be left with if his work fails?"

I have to actively work to keep my eyes from going wide. This is a lot of information to take in, and my daughter is not the right person to process it with. I try to sidestep the Reid of it all. "Have you ever thought about that? Me or Dad eventually being with someone else?"

"Sometimes." She shrugs. "Honestly, my first reaction is that it feels weird."

"Well, you did tell me that you didn't want my heart to get stomped on again."

She looks at me thoughtfully. "I did say that, didn't I?"

My gaze narrows at her. "Did you not mean it?"

"No, I definitely meant it. I told you, the sad mom thing is no fun for me, to be quite fucking—sorry—honest. I love you, but you ruined banana bread for me forever."

I laugh. The months following the divorce were a haze of sugar and flour, me feverishly flipping through my mother's cookbooks with religious fervor, as if the power of a perfectly fluffy pavlova could save me from myself.

"I really did believe in the healing powers of baked goods," I admit.

"But when I get past the weirdness," Emme says, "I actually think it could be good for you to have another person in your life. Someone your own age." She eyes me for a moment, then looks back down into her mug. "Also, like—I just don't want to be the reason why you don't move on."

That she worries about fucking up my life like I worry about fucking up hers—it's too much to bear. My first instinct is to deny the situation entirely: Who says I haven't moved on? And who says I need to be in a relationship to prove that I have?

But that instinct alone tells me she's right. Maybe I have been keeping Emme too close, using her as a shield to protect myself.

To Emme, I say, "I'll take that under consideration."

Then I put on a smile and suggest we have a couch day, which is probably not the most tactful move, but Emme takes me up on it happily. We watch *The Fellowship of the*

Ring, her comfort movie, pausing to order lunch from the diner and take an online quiz determining which *Lord of the Rings* character we are. (Galadriel for me, Frodo for Emme.)

By the time the movie's over, it's late afternoon. I'm about to ask her what she thinks she wants to do for dinner when she suddenly sits up from where she's been lying on the other end of the sofa. Her expression is inquisitive yet determined, a woodland creature emerging from a long hibernation.

"Is it too late to go to the show tonight?" she asks.

I check my watch. "If we hustle, we can make it. What made you change your mind?"

"I think I was holding out hope that Dad would suddenly turn around and tell me that he could take me. But now I feel like that's never happening."

Her words hang heavily between us. She doesn't speak them with malice, or even much sadness, but to my ears, they are laden with melancholy. I realize that this is exactly the kind of behavior she saw from me with James: All this sitting around, waiting for him to do *more*. Be present. Care. And the disappointment when he never did.

Emme shrugs. "I'm just not going to make what he did worse by putting myself in time-out because of it."

This is not the first time Emme has casually doled out a nugget of profound wisdom, but this one hits hard. *I'm just not going to make what he did worse by putting myself in time-out because of it.* I turn it over in my head until it sticks.

Emme pushes the blanket off her, arches her back into a long, luxurious stretch, then bounds up the stairs, announcing that she'll be wearing a babydoll dress and sneakers to the show tonight, in honor of Juliet.

I follow her upstairs to shower and change. I check my phone, which I've successfully avoided for the past four hours.

The screen is lit with texts and a missed call from Hayes, my agent. I skim the barrage: There's an opportunity with *Resonance*, a major music magazine. The project would be a series of portraits of up-and-coming musicians. Hayes threw my name into the ring, and now I'm under serious consideration for the contract.

I call him on speaker while I pull out an outfit to wear to the show.

"They need an answer by Tuesday at three," Hayes says. I can almost hear him pacing. "That's two days. Less, considering that it's almost five, and I've been calling you since noon."

"I can see that," I say. "I was working on images from the Jeff Buckley thing this morning, then spent the day with Emme." As if I need an excuse.

"The Jeff Buckley thing being the free thing? Which you took without consulting me?"

Playful condescension drips off his tone. But I adore this man—and his pragmatic approach to creativity is what makes him the best person to have in my corner. He's the kind of person I would hate to have on the other side of the negotiating table.

"Some of us are actually willing to do things without getting paid for them," I say.

"And I will never understand you people."

He's downplaying his generosity. In the throes of my divorce, Hayes took it upon himself to come over every week with martinis, omakase, and a lineup of movies he dubbed "the Bitchfest," starting with *Death Becomes Her* and *All About Eve*.

He ditches his snide tenor. "So there have been some developments here. After the initial portraits in New York, they want you to follow three of the bands on tour for one month each—July, August, and September—and those images would run in sequential issues."

"That's . . . wow."

"Yes. It is very wow." I drop onto the bench at the end of my bed. When I don't answer for a few seconds, he jumps in, "Tell me what you're thinking about."

I am genuinely shocked by this offer—I've photographed plenty of musicians and live shows over the years, but I don't have any experience as a tour photographer. Being embedded with performers that way is a whole thing—and it's never paid my bills.

"What's the compensation?" I ask.

"I'm going to be straight with you, the compensation is not up to our usual standard."

When he tells me, I physically balk. "I'm worth more than that." After decades of objective success in this field, I've come to adopt what Hayes refers to as the Average White Male Mindset: knowing your worth and asking for that or more, without agonizing or hand-wringing.

"I know you are, and believe me when I tell you I am

working on this. But you know I wouldn't be encouraging it if I didn't think it would open you up to an entirely new audience, and push you creatively. It's the kind of work you actually want to be doing, if I can be so bold."

Hayes is one of my staunchest supporters, but over the past few months, he has been subtly pushing me to expand beyond my artistic comfort zone—hence putting me forward for this gig without my knowledge, let alone my express permission. And he's right: This job would solve the problem of my next long-term project, and it would allow me to access the type of photography I haven't gotten to tackle, in earnest, for years.

"That aside." My mind drifts to the Jeff Buckley selects I did this morning, the delight of seeing moments in the photos I didn't even register in person. "Why do they want *me* to do this? Aren't I too old to go on tour? Aren't there thousands of wildly talented twenty-year-olds who should be doing this instead?"

"Well, if you don't take it, then a twenty-year-old *will* take your place. But they want you because you have style, you have experience, and you'll lend an air of legitimacy to this publication. And we know they sorely need to reclaim that after their . . . TikTok-ification. Which is what you get when you hire a toddler to do a grown-up's job."

He's referring to the newly minted twenty-eight-year-old editor-in-chief, who was until recently the magazine's social media director. The brand had been languishing in respected near-obscurity for a decade—whatever is the equivalent of an elderly animal retiring to the woods to die in peace, as Hayes put it—until her social strategy revived the brand, introduced it to a new generation of readers, and returned it to profitability through a smart combination of influencer marketing and good old-fashioned targeted ads.

"Well, I do want to join the fight against the TikTokification of legacy publications," I say. "But you know that's not the most important factor here. I can't leave Emme for three months."

"Well, thank goodness this aligns with her summer break, give or take a couple weeks in September."

"Yes, but I can't have her gallivanting around the city unsupervised all summer long."

"I'm sorry to share this news with you, sweetheart, but she does have another parent."

"Who has a terrible track record with honoring his personal commitments."

"Lili, you have never asked that man for anything. Just force him to take on some of the child-rearing responsibilities for once in his life."

I have to admit that the risk-taking part of me, the part I've kept under lock and key for so long, is begging me to do this. And James and I—I wouldn't call it a breakthrough, but he did just demonstrate *something* in communicating with our daughter.

The thought occurs to me that Reid would be a good person to talk to about this.

I blow out a breath and get up from the bench. We need to leave soon if we want to make it to the show.

"Give me a little more time to consider this," I say.

"Of course. Until Tuesday at three," Hayes says.

Then he hangs up, and I stand there with my phone in my hand. I flip back to my text conversation with Reid. Our exchange is short, but I scan over it again and again, and each reread gives me another delicious hit of possibility.

I type out a text, delete it, type it out again.

How was the Met?

I hit send.

Then I drop my phone on the bed like it's a live bomb and escape into the shower.

When I come back into the bedroom after I'm dressed, I gingerly pick it up, afraid of what I might not find.

Gracie lasted about three minutes. Must be a record for least time spent at any single museum.

This time, I don't hesitate before texting him back.

You could've redeemed yourself with a trip to the Natural History Museum. Everyone loves the gem hall.

I allow myself a moment to dwell on the memory of the two of us making out in one of the dark, sheltered corners, so far away from the throngs of visitors that we felt as if we were in a private room. Then again, we always felt that way.

Why are these rocks making me want to fuck you so badly? Reid had whispered, coming up for air.

Everything makes me want to fuck you so badly, I'd responded.

Now I feel my face flush, remembering how bold I once was with him. How could that have ever been me? Where did that version of myself go?

And how can I be that free, that brave, again?

Well, you and I loved the gem hall, Reid texts.

I startle when I hear a knock on my door, more of a warning than a request for permission. Emme comes in a half second later, wearing one of my velvet skater dresses from the nineties and a pair of high-top sneakers, her space buns freshly wound and spritzed with a fine sheen of pink glitter. She plops down next to me on the bed and leans her head on my shoulder.

"Who are you talking to?"

I turn my phone over in my hand. My first instinct is to deflect, tell her it's no one. And then I remember I resolved not to do that anymore.

"Reid," I say, feeling a little like a caught teenager.

"Mm-hmm." She gives me an honest-to-god knowing smile. "Thought so."

I laugh. "Why is that?"

"You're doing a . . . thing. With your face." She taps the back of my phone with an iridescent blue nail. "And you hid your phone, which makes me think *something* is going on here."

"OK, Sherlock." I stand and toss my phone in my bag. "Let's go."

At the show, my attention keeps faltering from the stage. I try to remain present, to appreciate the bombastic pop covers and the cotton-candy set, but my mind keeps doling out snatches of Reid. The way his breath felt against my throat. The buttery-smooth sensation that slid over my skin when I got him to laugh. The uncontrolled, helpless sound he made when he slipped his fingers into me, somewhere between a groan and a sigh.

Intermission offers a gust of relief from the fantasies unfolding in my head. I'm finally able to wrangle my focus during the second act, but then it's like the memories animate my physical form: My knee bounces, my fingers fidget. By the time Juliet bursts into a power-ballad rendition of ". . . Baby One More Time" after finding Romeo dead, I'm restless with unspent energy.

I pull out my phone to check my texts as soon as the curtains close. When we rise for a standing ovation, Emme shifts her hip to press against my leg.

"Mom," she says, "you're insufferable. Just go see him."

From the set of her mouth, I know she means it.

I really do want to see him, but the concept of going on what would amount to a booty call feels truly preposterous.

"It's late," I say.

"It's nine twenty-seven," Emme responds.

"I don't even know if he wants to see me."

Emme looks at me like I'm truly missing the point. I don't blame her—I can hear what I sound like as I give these petty excuses, but I can't seem to stop myself from rattling them off.

After we're herded out of the theater, we head east to avoid the cab-seeking crowds. We're just about to cross Park when Emme stops me and takes out her phone. To my surprise, she actually puts it to her ear to call someone.

"What's your dad doing right now?" she asks into it.

A garbled response on the other end. I am paralyzed by shock. And a little bit of fear. And then, an awed respect.

"Yeah, she definitely does."

Another unintelligible response.

"OK, she can be there in fifteen minutes."

Then Emme takes my hand, leans out into the street, and promptly hails a cab. She opens the door for me and nudges me into the backseat.

"You're going to meet Reid at the bar at the Mark Hotel. Have fun, be safe, bye!"

Before I can say a word, she slams the door shut. The taxi peels away from the curb, hurtling uptown. I barely have a moment to react to what just happened when my phone buzzes in my hand.

Reid: Emme asked you to meet me at the bar, right?
Lili: She didn't ask me. She ordered me.
Reid: Don't go to the bar. Come to my room.
Reid: 318

Twenty minutes later, my heeled mules press into cream-colored carpet, muffling my approach. The hush of the gardenia-scented hall makes me feel as if I'm sneaking off to an assignation—which, I suppose, I am.

I pause in front of the door. I am keenly aware that this

moment represents a distinct *before* and *after*: I can still turn heel, jump in a cab, head home, and be in bed before eleven, like nothing ever happened.

But then, maybe we're already in the after. Maybe Reid and I have always been in the after.

I force myself to stop thinking and knock on the door.

XV

When Reid opens the door, he takes me in the same as I do him, openly, hungrily. The sleeves of his shirt are rolled up, revealing the softened leather of his watch around his wrist, and I think back to the first time I saw him, the assumptions I made as I misinterpreted his cheap suit and scratched timepiece. How *young* I was. How much more I know now, and how confused I still am.

Reid inclines his head. "Come in." When he notices me glancing around the room behind him, he adds, "Gracie's staying a few doors down."

I follow him in. We both know what's happening here, and with the liberation of pretense, I feel myself grow deliciously lightheaded, like I've just drunk a column of champagne. Behind me, I hear the *snick* of the door shutting. The room is all elegant creams and grays, ensconced in warm light. There's a small sitting area in the far corner, two plush-looking armchairs facing a low, round marble table with a single pristine pink rose in a crystal vase in the center.

I settle into one of the chairs, consciously avoiding the gravitational pull of the bed in the middle of the room.

"Can I get you a drink? All I have to offer is whatever's in the minibar. Or room service, if you want," Reid says, crossing the room.

"Whatever's in there is good. Now that I've gotten myself here, I don't want interruptions."

Reid laughs—a low, knowing sound. He crouches down to open the minibar, and I home in on the way he rests his wrist on his folded leg, the flex of his thighs beneath the fabric of his pants. Every inch of my skin has been charged since last night, my nerve endings buzzing like live wires.

He turns to look at me over his shoulder. "Lili?" He catches me staring. I see the glint of it in his eyes.

I must have missed the part where he asked me what I wanted. "Is there whiskey?"

"Neat?"

I nod.

Handing me a highball glass, he sits in the chair across from me and cradles his drink in the palm of his hand. Then he just . . . considers me. When I take a sip, I feel the burn of the whiskey in my chest, the burn of his eyes tracing down my neck.

"You chose a nice place to stay," I say. I can't bring myself to articulate anything of substance. I can't verbalize anything I'm thinking without opening the floodgates.

He clears his throat, rousing himself. I am so aware of his awareness of me. I am expansive with possibility. I wonder if this is what performers feel the moment they step onto the stage, as if every single molecule in the room is reorienting around them.

"It's a little much." He smiles and shrugs. "But the Upper East Side still feels like the quintessential New York dream to me, and I wanted to show Gracie that." His voice has gone soft. "And also—where I lived when I lived here. A bit of a nostalgia play, I guess."

"Is your uncle still on Eighty-Eighth?"

"He died in 2017. Cat sold the apartment. But I still associate this neighborhood with him. It's . . . gentlemanly. Dignified."

"I'm sorry, Reid."

He takes a sip of his drink. "He was closing in on ninety and passed peacefully in his sleep. It's sad, but not tragic. Cat's words, not mine. But, you know. I am someone who knows the difference."

I hum in agreement. I shift in my chair and slip off my shoes, folding my legs underneath me. I see Reid tracking the movement with his eyes.

"How's your mom?" I ask.

"Living her best life in Santa Monica. She's spending most of her time painting and taking long walks on the beach."

"Sounds like she's 'romanticizing her life,'" I say.

He laughs. "Main character energy, for sure."

He watches me take another drink, and every cell in my body is screaming for him to keep looking at me like he is, to touch me with his strong, sure hands, but continuing to avoid the little tiff we had last night feels like a lie, and that's not the precedent I want to set. Not with Reid.

"So," I say. "What I said before you left—"

Reid holds a palm up. "Lili, it's fine. We don't need to get into it again."

I eye him sharply, curious about this reaction. Why is he deflecting? It's been the other way around—him pushing me to be honest and me ducking around it.

"I think we do," I say, and it comes out more easily than I expect. "I need you to know that I was reflecting on my own insecurities. I know that I'm hung up on my behavior in my marriage—I honestly can't believe how well you probably grasp that already—and I see the mistakes I'm making in co-parenting. But I'm also punishing myself, and last night, I was punishing you. There's just a lot I want to do better." I move forward in my seat, urging Reid to meet my gaze. Reid sits back in his chair, breaking our eye contact.

My heart hits my throat, and the words rush out. "You're just . . . you're the best person, Reid."

He raises an eyebrow. "You might be a little deluded about me, but I'm flattered."

"I'm not deluded," I say, laughing. "I am entirely objective."

"Objective." He takes a deep breath. "I'm sorry I unloaded my whole sob story on you yesterday. I think I do a pretty good job of keeping myself on lock, but sometimes the past . . ." He gives me a smirk, and I feel a breath of relief. "There's something about seeing you that cracked something open, I guess."

My phone dings, and I curse under my breath. "I'm sorry." I reach down to fumble inside my bag for it. "Let me just see if this is Emme."

I find a text from Hayes. *Hearing that Resonance is considering someone else for the project. Petra Collins type, but somehow even younger. Thoughts?*

I shake my head, slot my phone back in my bag, and take a long sip of my drink. Over the twelve years I've been working with Hayes, I've learned his moves: He's going to find every excuse to be in my ear and try to force my hand.

"All good?" Reid asks.

I nod. "Not Emme. She's probably deep in a smug, satisfied sleep. It was my agent."

Reid cocks his head.

"There's a potential job that came out of left field. I'm not sure if I can take it."

When Reid dips his chin, silently prodding for more information, I give him my take: the unexpected opportunity of it, the countless complications, and the fact that they'll move on and never give me a second thought if I say no.

"It sounds incredible, Lil," Reid says.

"It sounds terrifying," I counter. "It feels so *big*. I don't know if I have room for this kind of thing in my life. I can't just disappear for three months and leave Emme to her own devices."

"You can't, or you won't?"

"I don't think there's a difference. Not at this stage."

"You know there's a difference." He leans toward me, and I catch a whiff of the whiskey, the scent of his skin—musky and clean, mixed with something that's distinctly him.

He swirls the liquor in his glass. "When I wrote *Mask of Sin*, I holed myself up in my friend's guesthouse in Ojai for six weeks over the summer. Gracie was nine. She stayed with Cat, and they'd come visit on weekends. She still maintains that that was the best summer of her life, which honestly hurts my feelings, but damn if it didn't prove to both of us that it's possible to be a good parent and also an artist."

I love the way his eyes light up, the same way they did years ago when he got animated about David Lynch or whether *The Godfather* was overrated. It's only when he shifts his weight in his seat that I see a question in his smile and realize I've been silently staring at him for a little too long.

"I like seeing you this way," I explain. "Talking about what you love. I'm a little jealous, actually. I want to feel that kind of drive again."

"You can. But you might—you might have to start taking some risks. I know you've made plenty of great art since having Emme. But I also get a sense that she might be your excuse to stick with what's comfortable."

"Did you feel that way? Before you wrote *Mask of Sin*?"

"I did, to be honest. I was getting to a point where I was just coasting, taking on projects I didn't believe in. Keeping my eyes on my bank account. I was providing security for Gracie, but I hated what I was ultimately modeling for her—what it looked like to give up on what you love." He sighs. "Honestly, the entire process of writing that screenplay was pretty painful. I hated it, at the time. I was totally alone, writing without a partner like I had for previous projects, worrying about my kid. And the potential for failure. And the distinct possibility that I was suffering from delusions of grandeur. But I would still take all that existential angst over the pain of not doing it. *Not* trying."

"You stopped making excuses," I say.

"I did."

"And that's how you won a fucking Oscar."

Reid drops his head and laughs. "That, and the three hundred other people who made that movie come to life." His eyes soften as they search mine. "You know, I remember the way you were when you were with your camera. It's like you became more of yourself. More confident and self-assured. More graceful, if that's even possible."

"Clearly you're not remembering the time I face-planted outside St. Dymphna's in my platform Mary Janes."

"Oh, I remember that. I also remember that you got up and immediately took a photo of your skinned knees. Hottest thing I'd ever seen."

I laugh. "I always felt like a braver version of myself behind my camera, when I was young. I kind of used it as armor. Like it could offer me access to people I would never be bold enough to approach on my own. But I wonder if as I've gotten older . . ." Something clicks for me. "I wonder if I've been using it more like a shield so people can't access *me*." Clarity builds inside me, like all the fragments of my anxiety have fused together to create a single, fortified force of will. I know that if I don't say yes to this job, that if I were to see another photographer's credit on this project, I would forever be haunted by what I chose not to do.

I look up at Reid. "Three months away still feels like too much." But as I say the words, the pieces begin to snap into place. "Maybe I can float doing the portraits here and following one band on tour for a month."

"If they want you enough, they'll make concessions. If not, at least you'll know you tried."

"Between James and my parents, I can figure out a situation that Emme's OK with."

"If Emme is anything like my daughter—and I've started to get the sense she is—she'll be more than OK with that." One corner of his mouth tugs up into a smile.

I groan, pressing a hand to my forehead, starting to process that I am actually going to say yes to this.

"It'll be great, Lili. If we don't do things like this now, when will we?"

"You're talking about this gig, right? Nothing else?" I bite back a smile.

"Of course. What else could I possibly be talking about?"

We share a charged look, and his eyes go sharper, clearer—set with determination. Anticipation. I watch his chest expand and fall beneath his shirt, and I'm overcome with a need to press my palms against it, to count the heartbeats beneath it.

When the tension pulls uncomfortably taut, I force myself to try to loosen it. To keep us talking for as long as I can stand. I wave my hand toward the window, gesturing at the city pulsing beyond it. “So what does Gracie think of all this?”

Reid sighs, runs a hand through his hair. “She loves it. She asked if we can stay an extra couple of days.”

A bubble of hope. “Can you?”

“We can’t, unfortunately. I’m in preproduction for a movie. Table reads start on Tuesday afternoon, so I have to head straight to the rehearsal space after we land.”

“Can I get the elevator pitch?” I ask, and I’m rewarded with that look again, the one that sets his eyes on fire.

“Four estranged siblings reunite to stage an intervention for their youngest sister, a tech billionaire struggling with an opioid addiction, but their secret motivation is to secure their places in her will,” he says. “The schedule’s nuts, but one of the perks of the award”—he rolls his eyes exaggeratedly—“is that I get to work with people who are the best at what they do. And the studios trust that we won’t entirely screw things up. The lead’s the oldest brother, and they cast Jack Felgate. He’s very British, has that effortless, approachable charm. It’ll make him a good villain.”

“You’re filming in the UK?”

“Georgia, for the tax breaks.”

“Ever think about writing something set in New York?”

He cocks his head at me. “Do *you* want me to write something that shoots in New York?”

“I’d like for you to get to the city more often.” I let myself express it without coyness or hedging.

“I’d like that too.” He hides his smile in his drink. Then he turns and looks out the window. “The dream of living here . . . never really left me." His gaze meets mine again, his eyes raking slowly down my body. "You know, if I hadn't gotten that letter from Jake, I would've stayed."

Suddenly, I am nineteen again, watching the morning sun dance across Reid's bare skin, wanting so badly to wrap my arms around him but telling him to go, instead. All at once, an alternate timeline plays out in my head: Reid never gets on a plane, we move in together, we are enormously happy, I never suffer the indignities of a low-paying job in a field that I hate, Reid finds a job he loves . . . and that's where the tape falters and rewinds.

"But if you didn't go back to LA, you might not have had the career you have now," I say. I know I'm right, but the words are sour on my tongue.

"But I might've had you."

My breath catches, but I force my next thought out. "But we wouldn't have our girls."

"I know." His voice is hoarse. "Therein lies the rub."

This is exactly where my own rewrite of history dead-ends every single time. If we'd both made different choices in the past, then the greatest miracles of our lives would never have come to fruition. And maybe we would've been happy in the alternate timeline, but we also might have crashed and burned, spectacularly—or worse, come to resent each other, slowly and then all at once. I shake my head at us, at this fool's errand of editing the past like we're in our own personal version of *Sliding Doors*.

I am here. Now, I tell myself. *Better instead to make choices today that I won't come to regret.* I want to get over my fear of all the things that could go wrong, of everything I could lose. And I don't want to talk about the complications of our lives anymore. I just want him.

I shift slightly in my seat so that I'm facing him head-on. I recross my legs. I'm in a black sweater dress that's ever-so-slightly too short, with a slit that rides up when I'm seated. Reid's gaze snags on that slice of bared skin on my thigh.

"It's been a really long time since someone touched me like you used to."

Reid gives me his upside-down smile—my comfort smile—and runs a hand down his face. "Fuck," he says, under his breath. When he looks up at me again, his voice is steadier, more controlled, but it has a hint of grit to it. "I still remember everything you like."

As if through his volition, my hand drops onto my knee and moves slowly up, a planchette on a Ouija board, coming to rest on my inner thigh. My skin is hot to the touch. I watch Reid's fingers flex and release on the armrest.

Any shyness I might have felt is shoved to the side by the force of my need and the warmth of the whiskey. I want him urgently.

"I kept imagining your hands on me, after you left last night," I say, "but I couldn't make myself feel the way you did."

I made myself come twice last night, and that did little to stifle the heat that's been building inside me since seeing him on that sidewalk two days ago. Because this isn't ambient lust. This is specific, personal. It's the rare alchemy of the past colliding with the present. I need to capture it while I can grasp it.

"Will you show me?" Reid asks. When I hesitate, he gestures at my hand with his glass. "Show me how you did it."

I drop my knees wider but shake my head. "I want you to finish what you started."

Reid is already lunging for me, his drink abandoned on the coffee table. He scoops me up with one arm and pulls me into his lap, and I collapse on top of him, our mouths opening hungrily against each other. It's less a kiss than a claiming, our tongues sliding against each other without finesse or technique, his hands scrambling up the back of my dress, both of us moved only by a desire to taste and touch as much as we can, while we still have the time.

XVI

Any lingering scraps of decorum vanish.

He pulls me closer until I'm straddling him in his chair, and that champagne-drunk feeling returns to me, the ecstatic lift, the promise of the drop. His hands roam my back, my neck, and finally drop down to my ass, sliding under my underwear and coaxing my hips to rock against him. A groan escapes his throat when I drag my nipples up the plane of his chest.

I stop for a moment and lean back, just enough to look at him. He has that hungry, glazed look in his eye. He moves to push the hair away from my face but stops to wrap a length of it around his hand.

"This hair," he says, like he's lost in me. "I've had dreams about this hair."

He gives it a light tug, just firm enough to show me his control. Then he releases me and stands, and my legs wrap obediently around him. I feel the insistent press of his cock against me when he walks us over to the bed, my hands sliding down his back as he lays me down onto it. Like yesterday, I realize, before we were interrupted.

Reid lets out a low laugh, like he notices this too. "Been here before."

I reach up to hook a finger inside the waistband of his pants. "Let's do it right this time, OK?"

That's all the permission he needs from me. With focused efficiency, he pulls the hem of my dress up to my clavicle, and I arch my back off the bed, helping him free it. He slides his warm hands over the sheer fabric of my bra, brushing his thumb over each nipple, as if to assure me he'll be back for them later.

When he drops down to his knees, my breathing goes thick and slow. He skims his thumb across my freshly painted toenails.

"Red," he says. Like he is cataloging every detail.

He grazes a kiss against my pinkie toe, then climbs up my body. He hooks his fingers around my underwear, fisting the fabric before pulling them down. He runs his hands along the backs of my legs and props my feet on the bed, my knees bent.

And then I am bared, split open in front of him. He lets out a little *hm* sound, and his hand kneads the back of his neck. His pause is just long enough that I can't help but wonder what he's thinking. But then he drops his head and presses a kiss to my inner knee, another on my thigh, and the pulse between my legs intensifies with each touch of his wet mouth against my skin.

Our eyes meet, and any kernel of insecurity dissipates when I see the sincerity in his face, his jaw tensing.

"I've wanted you for so long." His voice comes out with a serrated edge.

"Me too."

"I want you again, Lili. All of you."

And then he dips his head and tastes me, with the kind of single-minded focus that threatens to tear me apart. My feet press against his shoulders, and my heels dig into the soft material of his shirt as my eyes flutter closed, every ounce of my attention zeroed in on where his tongue laps at me, where his fingers begin to move inside of me. I open my eyes long enough to see that he's palming his cock through his jeans, and the fact that he's hard from this, from the taste of me, is too much for me to bear. My orgasm rushes out of me, like it was hovering too close to the surface. I go lightheaded as the shock waves subside, and I need him on me, against me, in me. To ground me. To bring me back to us and keep me there.

I claw at the back of his head, tugging him up to meet me. He presses himself entirely against me, our torsos lining up. Still fully clothed, he bucks against my pulsing core, and with the friction, the weight of him, the desperation in his expression . . . I'm so close to coming again. If he grinds against me one more time, I will.

"I need to be inside you," he says into my mouth.

"I have never needed anything more in my life."

I feel his laugh vibrate against my chest. Quickly, he scrambles out of his pants, I slide off his shirt, and then I lie back again. I reach into the space between us to stroke his hard cock once, twice, and he lets out a deep, strangled groan. Before I can guide him into me, he shifts back onto his heels, bracketing my ribs with his hands.

"Are you . . . can we do it this way?"

"I'm honestly not sure. The joys of perimenopause."

Reid drops a kiss on my temple. "Give me a second." He retrieves a condom from the minibar. He smirks. "When I saw these in there, I actually laughed out loud."

When he positions himself over me again, it's as though the anticipation has had a chance to redouble.

"OK, I . . . fuck," he breathes.

"I know." I lift my head to catch his lip between my teeth and draw him down to meet my mouth. I taste myself, mixed with bourbon and mint, on his tongue. I taste everything he's trying to say but can't seem to find the words for: The loneliness, the longing, the years of wondering. The relief. The pure, unadulterated joy.

Then he rests his forehead against mine and moves into me with a single, perfect thrust. There is a finality to the fit of him. This, us, is inevitable. Nothing about how it feels for us to join is surprising—we have been together before—yet somehow, it's still exactly the same and so, so much more. I grasp my hands on either side of his jaw and tilt his head to make eye contact with me, silently seeking verification that he is as dumbstruck as I am by this moment, by the implausible familiarity and intensity of it. His small, silent nod is my answer.

Reid grips the undersides of my thighs, pulling me wider as he moves steadily inside me. My hands explore the surprisingly soft skin of his back, relishing the power of his movements. The ache builds and expands inside me, scrabbling for release. I press my mouth into his neck, taking his sweat onto my tongue. His thumb drops between us to my clit.

"I think I'm going to come again," I hear myself sob into his skin. For some reason, I feel like I need his permission to let go this time.

With one hand, he holds the side of my face, coaxing it away from his neck so he can look at me. He keeps a light hold of my chin with his forefinger and thumb, keeping my gaze fixed on him. His movement slows.

"Yes, baby," he says, with a brutally slow thrust. He slips his thumb into my mouth. "I want you to come for me."

He picks up a steady pace. My thighs squeeze around him, and my back arches against the bed. My vision goes white, and I break apart underneath him, completely overcome with the fact that this is him, this is Reid. My dream boy.

And from the way his gaze searches for me, I sense he's thinking the same thing. In the intensity of the moment, this shattering of the timeline between the past and the present—and between now and a murky, unknowable future—I feel that fearless part of myself threaten to close down again.

I hold his face in my hands and try to wrench myself back open, to stay in the present. I am exquisitely, painfully aware of all my warring emotions as Reid comes inside of me with a few final thrusts. He collapses into me and his hands tangle in my hair, his fingers playing against my scalp in gentle, subduing strokes. When our breaths begin to slow, he peels himself off me and props himself up on his forearms. His gaze is clear and bright and steadfast against mine.

"Hi," he says.

My chest floods with warmth, but that tiny, warning voice that retreated when Reid opened the door for me rears back into my head.

This is a fiction, it says. *This cannot last.*

I run my thumb over his swollen bottom lip, then take it between my teeth, just to shut myself up.

"It's you," I say, breathing the words into his mouth.

XVII

An hour later, I'm wrapped in Reid's T-shirt, the scent of him mingling with the neroli-and-pepper fragrance of the hotel body wash emanating off my skin. Reid is sitting up in bed next to me, and his hand is absentmindedly stroking my thigh over the sheets as he checks his email on his phone. He was supposed to read over some notes from the director tonight. "Before you came here and ruined my plans," he said with a smirk.

I haven't felt like this in years. It's not just the sex (though, god, the sex) but this easy intimacy afterward. Reid lifts an arm, and I curl into him. It's almost a reflex, simple and unfussy, as though I'd learned it over thousands of nights just like this.

It was never like this with James. Even in our prime, we retreated to opposite sides of the bed after sex.

Is it possible to let this thing with Reid grow into something? The thought blooms in my chest, tentative and hopeful. Maybe we can find a path forward. Maybe I can be brave enough to try.

But then my eyes drift to his suitcase, already half

packed. The hotel key card on the dresser. Everything that points to how fleeting this moment is, that we're borrowing time we don't really have.

And now I feel it—that dangerous jolt into something beyond simple affection. It threatens to rearrange my priorities, to upend the careful architecture I've built since my divorce. What happens if that tremor becomes an earthquake, toppling the life I've constructed?

But if I stop this now, maybe we can both walk away intact.

"I'm panicking," I say suddenly, "and I don't know why."

Reid looks up from his phone, then sets it aside, and I watch his expression shift into concern. "Let's talk about it, then."

His kindness makes it harder, somehow. James would have sighed, told me I was being dramatic, and gone back to his phone. But Reid turns his attention to me, waiting.

I take a deep breath to shore myself up for what I need to say. But then I shake my head, like I'm trying to rattle something loose. I want to stop trying to craft a perfectly nuanced and diplomatic response. I want to tell him exactly how I feel, despite how hard it is to translate those feelings into words.

"I care about you so much," I blurt out, "and I don't want to not see you again."

Reid gives me a smile. "Sex was that good, huh?" I nudge him gently, and he catches my hand. "Hey. I feel the same way, Lili. Seriously."

"So you would want to keep in touch?"

He laughs softly. "I would want to do more than keep in touch."

"OK." I take a deep breath and try to let it out slowly. I'm still lodged too far inside my panic to appreciate what we just admitted to each other. "And it's not freaking you out at all? How suddenly this all happened?"

"Is it sudden? I would argue we're three decades late."

"Right." I hold his hand tighter, as if to steady myself. "But how would we make this work? We live three thousand miles apart."

"That's what planes are for."

"So we fly back and forth across the country until . . . what?"

"Until we find a place to land."

"What about the girls?" The more granular this discussion becomes, the more my heart races. "We can't uproot their lives. And what about our parents, and our work?"

"We can figure out the logistics," Reid says. "Lili, these are all solvable problems if we want to solve them."

The way he says it, so matter-of-fact—it terrifies me, because I understand he's right. I know these aren't real obstacles; they're excuses. And the fact that he can see right through them so easily, that he won't let me hide behind them, makes me feel more exposed than I have in ages.

For years, I could disappear behind the smoke screen of my arguments, free to talk myself into my anxieties without any pushback. But Reid sees everything. He sees that I'm afraid of making the wrong decision again, of dragging my daughter into yet another heartbreak.

But that doesn't make my feelings any less present.

"Long distance doesn't work," I say. "It didn't work for us the first time." And there it is: The thing we've never discussed.

"We didn't even *try* long distance the first time, Lili. We were just kids. We had no idea how to handle each other then."

"And now we're adults, and our lives are so much more complicated. I honestly don't know if I'm strong enough to withstand another heartbreak. I need to be functional, and I will not be functional if you break my heart. There's too much at stake."

Reid is searching for me, trying to make eye contact. I know he wants me to face him head-on, but I can't do it. A door has shut inside of me.

"I want to be with you now," Reid is saying. "Believe me, I understand how scary it feels to embark on something like this at this stage in life, with everything we've lost. But have some faith in my feelings for you, OK?"

"Why would I have faith in that?" The words tumble out before I can stop them. "We loved each other then, when we were young and free and had nothing other than distance getting in the way. And you still left. *I* still left. What makes you think we can make this work now?"

Reid runs a hand through his hair. I know he's trying to stay patient, but his voice rises in pitch, frustration cracking his facade. "Yes, and you think I haven't considered that? That I haven't spent the last thirty years thinking about you, looking for you in other people? Wishing that I'd tried harder to hold on to you when I had the chance? So I think"—his hands drop to his lap—"I think we make this work because we *have* to, Lili. We have to try."

Hearing him say this makes me panic more. His confidence, maybe. That he seems so buoyed when I feel like I'm drowning. So I start swimming harder against the current, because I don't know what else to do.

"I don't know why you would trust me," I say. "I chose James, and that was a disaster. I *knew* it was a disaster, and it still took me years to get out of it. What if I'm the problem? What if I'm just not equipped to bc in a relationship?"

Reid takes off his glasses and pinches the bridge of his nose. He looks tired, wrung out. "I'm sorry for what you went through with James, and I have to assume you contributed to the problems in that relationship. Because that's how relationships work. But I'm not him. *You're* not only ever going to be who you were in that marriage."

"I have a proven track record of mishandling relationships, and I don't want you to become collateral damage. Or Gracie. Or Emme, yet again."

"Didn't you just tell me you didn't want fear to rule your decisions anymore?"

"There's a fine line between fear and intuition." I dig my heels in, unwilling, unable to stop myself. "Maybe we do try this, and six months from now, you decide that it's too complicated, or *I'm* too complicated, and we realize that this was just a fantasy that was never meant to be real. Maybe the smarter choice is to stop now, before we hurt each other again."

I'm being cruel now, and I know it. Reid's face changes, and I can see him trying to process how we got here so fast.

"Hold on." He shifts in the bed like he can't get comfortable. "How did we go from talking about plane tickets to you deciding this is doomed?"

"I'm being realistic," I say.

"You're spiraling."

I let out an exasperated laugh. "We can't even have a conversation about logistics without falling apart."

"Because we're not talking about logistics!" Reid snaps back. He stands abruptly and moves across the room, leaning in front of the window, like he needs to physically distance himself from this situation. From me. When he speaks again, his voice is lower, more intense. "You're scared, and instead of being honest about it, you're talking yourself out of this before we've even started."

His words hit me like a slap. I know he's right. Someone is finally seeing me clearly, and despite that—because of that—he's deemed me worth the risk. I *am* scared of how much I want this, and how easily I'm able to sabotage it.

And doesn't that prove my point exactly? "I'm trying to consider what's best for everyone involved," I say, and I can hear how righteous I sound. "Not just follow my feelings off a cliff."

Reid stares at me for a long moment. "Nothing I've said has gotten through to you. Right now, it doesn't seem like anything will."

His resignation stops me cold. He's giving me an out, exactly like I asked for. But now that I have it, the victory feels like a fistful of fool's gold. I'd thought it was worth something to me, but now I can see its cheap sparkle, feel its flimsy weight.

"Reid, I—"

"Lili, just . . . stop." There's something dejected in his voice that I haven't heard before. "You win. You're right. This might just be too complicated to navigate, and I'm not going to beg you to try."

I look at him now, the way defeat sits in the hollows of his cheekbones and the heavy set of his shoulders, like they're bearing a persistent weight. Clarity pierces me: I got my way, I found my escape hatch, and now it's like I'm in a free fall. Now I would beg him to forget the words I said that made him look like this. But I see on his face that I've pushed too hard, made too big a mess of this. I can't take it all back now. Can't make him believe me.

Ultimately, my fear and exhaustion overtake my regret. I get out of bed and dress in the bathroom, my hands shaking as I put on my clothes. I catch my reflection in the mirror—my swollen mouth, my smudged mascara—then quickly look away.

I sit on the edge of the bath, holding on to Reid's T-shirt. The fabric is soft from years of wear and washing. It smells like the essence of him. I press it into my face, then draw it away. What right do I have to seek solace in him, even this small part?

None. Not after what I just did.

I should go back out there, I think. *I should try to make this right.*

But then: Shouldn't I trust the instinct that warned me to pump the brakes? The thought surfaces like a life raft. We *were* moving too quickly. Getting too wrapped up in the idea of what we might be without thinking clearly about the reality.

I fold the T-shirt and leave it on the low stool next to the bathtub. When I come back into the bedroom, I try to avoid looking toward where he sits at the edge of the mattress with the heels of his hands pressing into his forehead.

I pick up my bag but fiddle with my phone before I turn toward the door, contemplating my next move. I can't leave without an acknowledgment.

"I'm sorry." It's the only thing I can come up with to say. "I really did think I could do better for you, but I . . ."

Reid looks up, and again I wish I could crawl back into the sheets and start this conversation over. But the distance between us has yawned open like a chasm.

"I'm sorry too," he says. "I thought we would both be willing to fight for this. At least I have my answer now."

The finality in his words breaks something in me.

I shut the door softly behind me and lean against it, trying to make sense of how quickly I just destroyed everything I might have had. I walk back down the beautiful, hushed hallway that, only hours ago, held so much promise. I press the button for the elevator. It dings hollowly in the empty space.

XVIII

I get home at almost one in the morning and feel simultaneously drained and wired. I crack open Emme's door to find her asleep. I text her to let her know I'm back so she won't worry when she wakes up. In my bedroom, I peel off my dress, slip into an old T-shirt and clean underwear, climb into bed, and stare at the ceiling. I try to quiet my mind. I pick up my phone and put it back down. Finally, I take a melatonin and fall into a fitful half-sleep, only to find myself awake after what seems like five minutes. I check my phone: It's 5:30 a.m.

My mind immediately flits to last night and replays my conversation with Reid in a torturous loop. I get out of bed and wash my face. I think about what my mother would say about the purplish half-moons under my eyes. I look at my single toothbrush in its narrow cup. I feel the press of tears. I text the only person who has any shot of freeing me from this cycle of self-pity.

Call me when you wake up, I write.

It's two-thirty in Seattle, but Nisha texts me back immediately anyway.

Call me now.

I do her one better and FaceTime her. I'm startled by my appearance on the screen, wan and slack, and if this were anyone other than Nisha, I would hang up immediately and pull myself together. But this is the woman who squeezed my hand during the first few hours of my labor contractions, who wiped the sweat off my brow and fed me ice chips until my husband finished his twelve-hour shift and took over for her.

"Can't sleep?" Nisha says when she picks up. She's in her parents' dimly lit kitchen, wearing her reading glasses and pajamas. A mug of tea hovers under her chin. I feel a surge of affection for my friend.

"I could say the same for you," I say. "Your hour is even more ungodly than mine."

"Menopause, baby. Because it's not enough to sweat through your underwear every two hours, they take away our sleep too."

"I'm sweating just looking at that tea."

Nisha taps the mug. "It's an ashwagandha-schisandra blend. You know it's bad when I'm turning to holistic measures to knock myself out."

"Why don't you get an Ambien prescription?"

"My love, Ambien stopped working for me twenty years ago."

We keep up like this for the next few minutes. Our small talk is a balm. Then I ask after Nisha's father, who's facing stage-four pancreatic cancer. He's being kept comfortable with medication and is at peace with his prognosis, she shares, and his acceptance has put her at peace too. But

Nisha's mother is taking it much harder, she tells me. As is so often the case with the ones who will be left behind.

"Now that we're off to a suitably morbid start to the day." Nisha takes a sip of her tea and crinkles her nose. "Tell me why your face looks like that."

I catch another glimpse of myself in the little square on my phone screen. As Nisha and I were talking, I slapped on a pair of sparkly gold undereye patches, and they've slid halfway down my face. I peel them off and squish the cushy gel material in my fist like a stress ball.

"Well," I sigh. "You're never going to guess who I ran into at the Jeff Buckley show this week."

I start with the girls' awkward meeting in the bathroom at Webster Hall and end with last night: How I'd had what very well might have been the best sex of my life, and how being with Reid was both new and familiar, like time had folded into itself. How I would forever be at a loss to explain the bizarre privilege of experiencing a decades-long dream come to fruition.

And then how I proceeded to destroy everything because my misplaced fear and self-doubt spiraled all the way out of my control. Because I'm too afraid to put myself out on the line and try this again.

Nisha is silent for a moment. "This is a lot to take in." She bites her lip. "How does Emme feel about all of it?"

"Considering that she and Gracie not-so-subtly engineered this whole thing, I'd say she approves of the idea of me and Reid." I pause for a beat. "The other day, she told me she doesn't want to be the reason I don't move on."

Nisha pouts and puts a hand over her heart. "Sweet girl."

"The sweetest. But she's getting caught up in the fantasy of it all. I don't blame her for that, but I have to be the grown-up here. I have to consider how much it will hurt her when this doesn't work out." I'm back to my talking points. The ones I spat at Reid and can't seem to keep out of my mouth.

Nisha laughs. "Hurts *her*? You're aware you're self-sabotaging, right?"

I can't help but laugh too. Nisha has a gift for getting right to the point. "Fully aware of that. Reid is too. He called me out on it."

"I'm quickly remembering why I liked him." Nisha blows out an exasperated breath. "James really did a number on you, Lil, and you're dragging all that into this thing with Reid. He was a good kid, and now he seems like a good man. A good man is hard to find, you know."

"Yeah. I've heard that one before."

I think back to my conversation with my mother, when I'd told her with such conviction that we don't have to let our pain rule us. Why have I reserved my compassion for others while keeping myself locked in the cell of my mistakes, cataloging every misstep, memorizing each one in painstaking detail, as though cocooning myself in them could prevent me from committing them again?

I hear a knock on the door. Emme comes in, her hair a staticky pink halo around her face. She climbs into bed next to me. Nisha beams when she sees her.

"You're up early," I say.

"I got your text and I wanted to come talk to you. How was last night?" Emme's voice is brighter than the time would suggest. Usually, she wouldn't get out of bed for another four or five hours.

I glance at Nisha. She smirks at me over her mug. *This is on you, babe.*

"We had a nice time, but I don't think Reid and I will be seeing each other again," I say.

Emme's face falls. "Why not?"

I smooth her hair behind her ear. "It's just too complicated. We both have a lot going on in our lives, and we live on opposite sides of the country."

"But that's what planes are for. Used intentionally, of course. I don't need to tell you they are a cancer to the earth."

That's what Reid said, I don't say.

Emme looks at me thoughtfully. Then she turns to Nisha. "What do you think?"

Nisha takes a pause so exaggerated, I wonder if she has somehow fallen asleep with her eyes open.

But then she nods. "You know, when your mom and I met on the first day of our freshman year, I thought she was the coolest person I had ever met." I give her a skeptical look—I've never heard her say this in my life. "I know you think I'm lying, Lil, but it's the truth." She looks back toward Emme. "She was so calm, cool, and collected, with her tastefully curated book collection and her little slip skirts and cropped cardigans. All her attention to detail, the way she protected her routines—I envied it. I was this sprawling mess, and she was this quietly interesting, mature city girl who had no problem leaving parties early and declining dates with guys if they were boring. She wouldn't let anything impinge upon her peace.

"But then, the summer before our junior year, she tells me that she's actually really unhappy. That the pressure of holding everything together is completely overwhelming, and she's so afraid that she's wasting the best years of her life chasing this idea of perfection. She's burnt out, we'd call it now. So, she asks me to help her figure out how to have fun. Real, genuine fun. You know what I tell her?"

"What?" Emme is rapt, and honestly, I want to ask Nisha the same thing: I remember that time, and I remember that feeling, but I cannot for the life of me remember this conversation.

"Get out of your own way and let yourself feel the good feelings. Obviously, your mom is a great student. She understood the assignment."

Nisha turns her gaze to me.

"So the next day, I take her to a tiny café on St. Mark's to go see this musician named Jeff Buckley. And then your mom meets this ridiculously hot guy and spends every minute of the next week with him, even though the new school year is about to start. She falls in love, and even though she never tells me those words herself, I know what love is when I see it. So, Emme, what's important in this story is not that the hot guy made your mom happy."

I watch Emme mask a grimace as she bravely weathers the news of her mom thinking a guy was hot.

Nisha gives us both her slyest smile. "It's that she *let* herself be happy first, and she stayed out of her own way long enough to make it count. And guess what? She still got straight A's the next semester. Maybe she was a little anxious, but her life did not fall apart because she let herself go for a second. Actually, her life *expanded*."

I return to that moment now, recalling with sudden clarity Nisha's edict to go forth and be free. Me coming home with that thrifted gunmetal slip dress and her telling me not to waste it. I swallowed her advice whole, stopped focusing on accumulating gold stars. I remember the way my summer had opened up—how I'd roamed downtown with my camera in hand, collecting freckles across my collarbone and stories that tumbled from my mouth at parties with a newfound ease.

And I realize, too, that if I had not embraced this mindset, I would have stayed home that night while Nisha sailed to Sin-é with another friend—maybe Trisha with the tinkling laugh or Monique with the bee-stung lips and the lilting Montrealer accent. And one of them would have noticed him: the boy in the freshly pressed suit, with hair that curled around his ears in the humid air that made everything else wilt. That night would not have belonged to me. Reid would have walked into someone else's story.

And here I am, thirty years later, still with so much to learn from that girl who was sometimes afraid but resolved to go forth anyway.

Here I am again, on the precipice of genuine connection, of freedom, of opportunity, and I'm running in the opposite direction of it all.

Nisha drains her mug and lets out a jaw-cracking yawn. "OK, this hippie shit is working. I'm gonna try to sleep for a couple hours before my parents get up. Love you girls."

"Love you, Neesh," I say.

Pale morning light seeps beneath the slats of the blinds, throwing stripes onto my rumpled bedspread. Beside me, Emme's breath is slow and sweet, and her long lashes cast shadows onto her cheek. She hooks a thumb underneath her stack of beaded bracelets and gently snaps them against her wrist. It strikes me that this is likely the moment when she's beginning to conceive of me as a whole person—with agency and hidden desires and an unfamiliar past—and not only as her mother. It strikes me, too, that this phenomenon might be more difficult for me to process than it is for her.

"I'm sorry that you didn't love Dad like you loved Reid," Emme says.

My chest hollows out. "I did love your dad—I really did—but I think what I felt for Reid was . . . less complicated. Reid just saw me for who I was. Does that make sense?"

"That must be a cool feeling."

"It *was* cool." Thirty years later, it still is. It's the vibrational attunement that also scares me. But I'm unwilling to share that fear with my daughter, to pass my cynicism down like a tattered heirloom. I want her to be aware of people's limitations, but I still want her heart to stay open in the way mine hasn't.

"I'm sure you'll experience something like that one day, if you want to," I say. "And I think it'll come easier to you than it did to me. You're already so much braver than I was. You don't need Auntie Neesh's pep talks to help you."

"I've always seen you as brave." Emme shrugs, like she didn't just short-circuit my brain.

I force Emme back to bed for a few hours, and when she wakes up a second time, I set out to model boldness—on one front, at least—and tell her about the *Resonance* job. I explain that we would work together to figure out a situation that feels right for her when I'm gone, whether that's staying with my parents or with James or some combination. Despite the risk avoidance that I showcased last night, I realize I do still want this job. That it's within my power to make this opportunity suit my life, or at least try to.

Still, it's not just *my* life, and I want Emme to have a voice. "But if you don't want me to do this—"

She cuts me off. "Mom." She rests a hand on my arm. "You know I'm not a baby anymore, right?"

I laugh. "I do and I don't."

"Well. Do."

I spend the next hour on the phone with Hayes, gathering as much information as I can about the project. Portrait sessions would take place in a month, tours would kick off right after, and no, I would not have to sleep inside a moving vehicle. I run my proposed plan by him: that I'll photograph all the bands here but follow just one on tour in August.

"And I want ten percent more in compensation," I add.

"Love that for you, but the comp is locked in. Trust me, I've pushed as much as I could while still retaining a scrap of dignity."

"Then I want to maintain copyright for my images and set up a gallery show." I sit up a little straighter, even though he can't see me. "And then I want to make a book."

"Well," Hayes says, and there is both venom and honey in his voice. "There she is. That is the smartest thing you've said in years."

When I hang up, I ride the momentum and do a deep dive into each of the acts I would be documenting. It's a motley group—one is a confessional singer-songwriter duo, another is a scrappy three-piece punk band outfitted in kilts and knee socks ("Like Dog From Hell without a rabies shot," a write-up says), and the last is a sultry, Wiccan-inflected shoegaze quartet. I'm a little surprised that I find all their music exciting, even groundbreaking, and I'm moved by the fact that every artist involved is a woman, which also makes the prospect of spending time on the road much more palatable.

An hour later, Hayes texts me: *They'll do it.*

"Yes," I say out loud. And then, "Fuck."

Forgetting myself, I open up to my messages with Reid—he's the first person I want to share this news with. My fingers hover over the keyboard, buzzing to type the words.

But I know I can't contact him. I'm the one who pulled that door shut.

When I head downstairs to share the plan with Emme, I pass behind her and see she's scrolling on Instagram. I can't help but peek at her screen when I glimpse an unmistakably familiar face, though the snow-white skin and impossibly shiny hair are in partial shadow. The geotag is Bemelmans Bar. Emme taps to Gracie's next story. This one shows three albums fanned out on a hotel bedspread. *Generation Records haul*, the text over the image reads. Next is the amethyst slab that lords over the entrance to the gem hall at the Natural History Museum, its hollowed-out core glistening and refracting in a way that makes my breath catch.

Surely, this is a coincidence. Surely, Reid is not intentionally retracing our steps, visiting all the spots I took him to thirty years ago. Surely, Reid is too hurt to reminisce about our shared past, to remind himself of the future we might have had together, had I not bulldozed right over it.

I muzzle the jolt of hope that gallops across my chest. *These are all New York institutions*, I tell myself. *Reid and I don't own them.*

But once again, I'm lying to myself. If I let myself be honest, this can only be one thing: proof that Reid is still searching for me. But this time, I need to find him.

Emme notices me, noticing her screen. She offers me the barest glance and casually swipes out of Instagram. "Busy day," she says.

XIX

In the afternoon, Emme comes into my office and tells me we need to do something fun. "To celebrate your music job thing."

I take a sip of my third cup of coffee. I've been holed up in here, pulling artistic references from my design library, cataloging the gear I'll need, and emailing with *Resonance*'s creative director to ensure our visions align.

Now I check the time on my computer: It's already close to two. I've been so consumed with the work and how much there is to do to prepare for this project, but I've also been avoiding the thing that is actually weighing down my conscience.

As soon as I shut my laptop, the argument with Reid barrels back into my mind. So does the full force of my regret. The finality of his words loops endlessly: *I thought we would both be willing to fight for this. At least I have my answer now.*

But those photos on Gracie's Instagram also won't leave me alone. Was Reid trying to channel something? Or was this just a farewell tour?

The hope and despair war inside me, leaving me paralyzed. I want to call him, to own up to my behavior and tell him that I don't just *want* to do better by him, but that I will. For him, I will.

I shake my head, trying to dislodge my thoughts. "What'd you have in mind?" I ask Emme.

She counts on her fingers. "Lunch. Vintage store. Another vintage store. Another vintage store. Bakery. Come home. *Lord of the Rings: The Two Towers*. Chinese food."

"I'm ready to go when you are."

"Give me fifteen minutes." She looks me up and down. "Is that what you're wearing?"

I let out a choked laugh. Mentally, I reevaluate my outfit: a pair of worn-in jeans, a white T-shirt, and my usual tangle of gold necklaces. "Yes, this is what I'm wearing. Is there a problem?"

"I think we should look cute today," she says. "This is a celebration. Maybe wear that blue top?" Then she steps closer to me, inspecting my face. "You could also use some blush."

I shoo her away, but when she leaves, I step close to the mirror hanging on my office wall. Unfortunately, Emme isn't entirely wrong—I still look drained. I head to my bedroom, slip into a cream silk camisole and a slouchy linen blazer, add a swipe of lipstick and a coat of mascara. Finish with the recommended blush.

When we meet downstairs, Emme gives me a satisfied smirk.

We walk toward the East Village, partly because the neighborhood has the highest density of vintage stores and bakeries, but also because even now, twenty years after moving out, I still feel magnetically drawn to my old stomping grounds. I may have grown up on the Upper West Side, but the East Village is where I became myself. When I lived here, I was on the edge of the rest of my life. When I come here now, I feel it still, even though, somehow, I have found myself in the middle of my life.

Emme emerges from the dressing room at a vintage store on Tenth Street in a calico minidress with a starched Peter Pan collar—the kind of thing my mother forced me into as a kid, but that looks perfectly irreverent on her. I wonder if she can sense the internal alchemy that arises when we're in this part of the city—the origami folding of my younger self into my older self. Part of me hopes that she can't, that I can keep this just for myself.

Emme tries on a few more things, and when we head back out onto the street, she's chatting about an audiobook she's been listening to about Indigenous plant medicine, and I realize we've rounded the corner onto St. Mark's and are heading east toward Tompkins Square Park. Emme's pace slows, and then she stops near the end of the block.

"Well," she says. "This is where I leave you."

"What?" We've only gone to two vintage stores so far.

Emme gestures to the building we're in front of. It's a cozy pub with a low green-and-white-striped awning and an outdoor seating area, where most of the tables are already taken. An hour from now, every streetery in the city will be packed.

Then it dawns on me: This was Sin-é's original location, before they closed in the mid-nineties.

"You're going in there," Emme says, "and I'm staying out here. I mean, I'm not gonna stand here the whole time, but you know what I mean."

"*Do* I know what you mean?" Then I feel my heart kick harder at my chest and my tongue go numb, like my body knows what's happening before my mind does.

"Do you trust me?" Emme asks.

"Of course I do."

She nods toward the door. "Go inside. I'll see you at home later."

I watch her turn and head in the opposite direction. After a few steps, she yells over her shoulder, "Enjoy your intervention!"

At one of the tables outside, a pair of twentysomething women sipping cold goblets of white wine are staring at me, and I can't parse whether their expressions hold amusement or judgment. Or just the detached curiosity that all New Yorkers eventually adopt. Still, their looks are enough to get me off the street.

Inside, the cool, dark air is a reprieve from the noise and heat. I haven't set foot in this building since '96, but it still feels charged with the promise of its former inhabitants, like Jeff Buckley's chords still reverberate off the walls. Near the door, there's now a built-in banquette and a few stools where I once sat on the floor in front of Reid. Where the mere presence of him at my back was almost enough to eclipse the legendary performance unfolding twenty feet from me.

And there, settled into the booth, is where I find Reid now. The light from the window emphasizes the salt in his hair, the burnished bronze of his skin. A glass of beer sits on the table in front of him. He looks up, and his expression opens when he sees me. We consider each other for several seconds, and the same sensation that I experienced when I saw him for the first time overcomes me: the uncanny inevitability of encountering this person here.

But now, I understand that fate will only chaperone you partway to your destination before it releases your arm. Right now, I'm choosing to take myself the rest of the way there.

I gesture toward the empty stool across from him. "Can I sit down?"

He gets up from the bench, and for a moment, I wonder if he's going to bail. I couldn't blame him if he did. But he puts a hand on my back, nudging me toward the seat he'd occupied, then takes the backless stool I'd just pulled out.

It's such a sweet, gentlemanly move, and I wonder whether I am going to start crying. I pull myself together and sit, aware of the distance he maintains between us.

A waitress comes over for our drink orders. I feel Reid's eyes skimming over me as I ask for an iced tea, but when I look back at him, his expression is shuttered. He's holding himself close.

"I'm guessing Gracie lured you here."

"Under false pretenses." His tone is carefully neutral. "She told me she wanted to have lunch here, let me order a beer, then bolted."

I can't help but laugh. "She didn't give you an excuse?"

The ghost of a smile crosses his lips, but it quickly disappears. "She told me she had cramps, because she knows I can't argue with that." He ventures a look at me. "How did Emme get you in here?"

"We were shopping in the neighborhood, and she kind of just . . . left me outside."

Reid shakes his head with the same mixture of admiration and exasperation that I feel toward my daughter. "Gracie would never admit it, but *The Parent Trap* is one of her favorite movies of all time."

"Emme's too." I sense an opening. "I have to say, though, I'm relieved. They kind of threw me a line. I've been wanting to reach out to you, to apologize for last night. I just . . ."

The waitress delivers my drink, cutting off my speech. After she leaves, Reid quietly surveys the room around us, once again deliberately avoiding my gaze.

"Have you been back here?" he asks.

I tamp down my disappointment. Reid doesn't want to hear my apology. Maybe he just needs more time—or maybe I really have messed things up beyond repair. But he's still here, talking to me, making a stab at conversation. That has to count for something.

"No. Nisha and I saw a show when Sin-é reopened on

Attorney Street in the early 2000s. It was great, but it just didn't have the same specialness this place did." I shake my head. "I don't know if this is overly dramatic, but I think when Jeff Buckley died, some of the magic of that time died with him."

"Yeah. We've changed a lot, haven't we?"

There's a pause while we sip our drinks. I hate the distance between us, the loss of our camaraderie and ease.

I want to get us back to where we were. I think of what Emme said about putting herself in time-out yesterday. I think of my younger self, too, her guileless zeal. And now, the complications, the fears, the hypotheticals . . . they're all flimsy when confronted with the sheer strength of my feelings for this man, my desire to have him again.

Reid clears his throat. "So what's happening with the *Resonance* gig?"

"They accepted the new terms."

For the first time since I sat down, Reid's face breaks into a smile, revealing the chip in his tooth I've come to find devastating. "That's amazing, Lili. You're taking it, right?"

Warmth floods my chest. Speaking it aloud to him makes it real. Historically, this is the point at which I would start second-guessing, but the anxiety has melted out of me. I'm no longer projecting into the future, mentally constructing an ideal version of myself and worrying about all the things I need to do to meet myself there. I'm content in this moment, relishing the accomplishment, happy that I get to share it with Reid. That I'm getting one more moment with him.

Reid, with his steady gaze, his soft T-shirt that drapes

easily over his broad shoulders, his hair that's a little more mussed than usual—maybe he didn't sleep well either—and the way he shifts in his stool to lean closer, waiting for my answer.

"I'm taking it," I say.

"I'm proud of you." The sincerity in his voice makes my chest tighten. "I'm glad you could figure it out."

Our eyes lock, and I can detect the ghost of another, truer meaning in his words: *At least you found a way through this one.*

"I'm learning that there are ways to figure these things out," I say carefully. "Mostly it involves getting out of my own way."

His laugh comes fast. It's like a summer thunderstorm, washing away some of the heat and tension, leaving everything clearer in its wake.

This, I think. I want more of *this*. Us. Now.

"Reid," I say, my voice steadier. "I'm sorry for giving up so quickly. Last night."

Reid's eyes lift from his beer. His expression is flat, but I notice a softening, a willingness to listen.

"What happened at the hotel . . . I was making excuses to deal with how scared I was. I wasn't just terrified of my heart being broken again. I was terrified of *you* being the one to break it. I care about you so much, Reid. I never stopped caring about you. So if things didn't work out again . . . it would hurt so much more. It's like we have this found time, and all I could think about was when it was going to run out."

Reid takes a breath, and his fingers drum against his glass. The silence stretches between us like a chasm.

"I should've called you out the second you started spiraling," he finally says. "I saw exactly what you were doing—trying to talk yourself out of this. And I just . . . let you." He runs his fingers through his hair, and the strands fall in a way that makes me want to reach over and smooth them. He looks out the window, like he's gathering himself. There's something raw in his expression when he considers me again, his walls torn down completely. His voice is lower, rougher. "I have to be honest, Lili. When you started listing all the ways this wouldn't work, all the ways we were doomed . . . a part of me believed you. I just thought . . . well, I fucked everything up with Thea. Why wouldn't I do it again?"

I see it in my mind: This being the end for us. Him breaking my heart at this bar. But now that's not the most frightening thing. Hiding myself from him—not throwing everything at this—is.

"I know," I say quietly. "I know I broke your trust. I intended to."

"I understand why you thought blowing this up was the safer route. I understood it as it was happening, but that didn't make it any less disappointing."

"Am I really so transparent?"

"To me, you are."

"That scares me, you know. I've been so used to hiding with people, and I wasn't ready for the exposed way I feel with you. But maybe that's exactly the point. To be able to be vulnerable without worrying about the other person bolting. It's what my parents have, it's what I experienced with you back then, and I think it's what I truly want—have always wanted—in a relationship. When I couldn't have it with James, I think I convinced myself I didn't really need it." I take a breath. "And then you showed up. Again. And you reminded me both of what I wanted and of what I'd lost. And . . . well, you saw what happened."

"I let you walk out last night. I shouldn't have, but I—" Reid starts. "After all the ways I failed Thea, I've been terrified to try this with someone else. So what you said, what you did . . . for a moment, it felt like I was right to let you go."

My eyes burn, and I have to close them. "I don't want to be the person who validates your fears. I can't promise I won't make mistakes, but I want to try. I want to show you that I can. And I have faith that you'll call me on my bullshit." I laugh. "But I think that might actually be what love is—being seen for exactly who you are."

He's quiet for a long moment, leaving my proverbial hat in my hand. But the distance between us seems to contract now, inching us closer together, bit by bit.

"I've wanted to see you for who you are since the night we met," Reid says softly, "but you haven't always let me."

"I'm letting you. I don't want to waste any more time hiding. Especially from you."

Reid laughs, the sound of a broken thing being mended. "Time is not one of our more abundant resources."

"But we still have enough of it. Right?"

When he looks at me now, I don't see the boy I once loved, the one who slipped into my life with a quiet determination and evoked so many novel urges in me: protectiveness, admiration, bone-deep need. I see this man, fortuitous and undeniable. It's like the shift from nostalgia to hope.

And I like this feeling more.

"Since we're doing this . . ." He rests his hands on the table. "Then I promise I won't let you walk out the fucking door again."

Relief washes through me. My whole body is flooded with it, with an understanding of just how precious his forgiveness is. "That is the most romantic thing anyone has ever said to me."

He looks at me intently. "If we're in this, we need to see it through. There hasn't been a day over the past thirty years that I haven't wondered whether I made the wrong decision when I went back home."

"You can't think that way," I say, even though I know exactly how he feels.

"I know I can't, but I still do. I understand that we needed to go through what we went through—butterfly effect, whatever—and yet I still wish it had happened differently. Let's not have to wish that again."

We look at each other for a long moment, and I push aside what we could have been and let in everything we still might be.

As if on cue, mine and Reid's phones both chime.

"I have a feeling I know who this is," Reid says, reaching for his.

Then he lets out a laugh that's unmistakably Gracie-induced—the kind that comes from being managed by your child.

I check mine and, unsurprisingly, find a text from Emme. *Stay out as long as you want. I'm w Gracie then sleeping at dad's. Good luck!!!!* 😈

"What's yours say?" I ask.

Reid angles his screen toward me. *don't eff this up. im going to babys all right w emme tn & you are not invited, sorry*

He laughs again when I show him mine. It's a small moment, inconsequential in the grand scheme of things, but it's like a preview into something larger. Into the future we'll build together. The girls commiserating, Reid and me happily caught in the crosshairs. The four of us tangled up in ways that feel exhilarating and comforting at once. Like joy itself. Like coming home.

Something shifts in Reid's expression, and the playful glint in his eye tells me he's envisioning the same flash-forward.

Then he sighs, runs a hand over his jawline. His shoulders drop, but not in defeat—it's like he's finally settling something heavy he's been carrying for a long time.

"I still have to fly back to LA tomorrow, Lil. I don't have a choice."

I reach for his hands, find them warm and solid.

"I know," I say. "But we'll find a place to land."

Stay for Lili and Reid's encore: Read the book's epilogue to find out where these two end up, and discover their essential East Village itinerary (plus, the '90s-era playlist to soundtrack your day). Just scan below or visit 831stories.com/foundtime.

More novellas like this one are waiting for you at 831stories.com, where we celebrate romantic fiction in all its forms. You can also dive into bonus content, products, events, fan fiction, and join our membership program to receive new releases early, get discounts across the site, and access all sorts of exclusive perks.

ACKNOWLEDGMENTS

Writing this novella has been one of the most joyful creative experiences I've had, and that is entirely thanks to Erica Cerulo and Claire Mazur. Thank you for the opportunity to be part of the 831 universe, for offering me more support than I could ever even think to ask for, and for being on Team Lili & Reid from day one. You are my romance heroes. Infinite gratitude to my friend, Alexis Cheung, for making the connection.

Thank you to Georgia Clark, whose early input was critical in helping me make sense of these characters. Jen Prokop, your edits turned my messy drafts into a capital-B Book. Working with you has made me a better writer. Sanjana Basker, thank you for your sensitivity read and your delightful commentary, which sometimes made me cry laughing. Thanks also to Madi Feller and everyone else at 831 Stories HQ for literally bringing this book to life. The definition of a dream team.

Thank you to every friend with whom I've had to reschedule plans so I could work on this book. Love you;

next dinner is on me. Thanks also to my friends and coworkers at theSkimm for supporting my writing life. I lucked out with every single one of you.

Tara Rosegarten, thank you for planting the seed and helping it grow. Dad, thank you endlessly for your love and wisdom. (Please skip chapters 4, 12, and 15.) Mom, no one on Earth believes in me like you do—you are my anchor. Alex, I couldn't do anything in life without you, including writing this book. Thank you for always getting what I'm going for and knowing how I can do it better. And thank you for gut-checking the smut. Who knew our Tessa Bailey obsession would end up here?

Jeff Buckley's music has been a constant in my life, and it has been my dream to pay homage to his magic in some small way. I listened to Jeff Buckley's catalog on repeat while writing this book, but I took special influence from his 1993 EP, *Live at Sin-é*. That, among other archival footage, formed the basis of Lili and Reid's first meeting. If you're interested in learning more about the real person behind the legend, I highly recommend Amy Berg's documentary *It's Never Over, Jeff Buckley*.

Finally, thank you to Jon, my California boy, for seeing me through the sticky spots and letting me use the detail of your chipped teeth. See you at the kitchen table tonight.

ABOUT THE AUTHOR

CAROLINE GOLDSTEIN is the author of *The Wayside* under the name Caroline Wolff, as well as the essays for the monograph *Transience* by Danielle L. Goldstein. She holds an MFA in fiction from NYU, where she also taught undergraduate creative writing. She is currently an editor at theSkimm and previously worked as an editor at Bustle. She lives in downtown Manhattan.

ALSO FROM 831 STORIES

Big Fan by Alexandra Romanoff
A high-profile scandal derailed Maya's DC career, and she's eager to fly under the radar—that is, until her former boy-band crush reaches out with a job offer.

Hardly Strangers by A.C. Robinson
One night with a rock star could upend Shera's best-laid plans, revealing how a chance encounter can rewrite a story—and change everything.

Comedic Timing by Upasna Barath
Naina is seeking a fresh start in NYC after breaking up with her girlfriend, but when she meets someone at a party, he's so offtype that her attraction to him fuels an identity crisis.

Set Piece by Lana Schwartz
When a breakout BBC star gets swarmed by fans during a night out, it's a no-nonsense bartender, CJ, who rescues him—and warms them both up for an after-hours hookup.

Square Waves by Alexandra Romanoff
The first spin-off in the *Big Fan* series, an enemies-to-lovers romance in which tabloid fodder mixes with a long-brewing rivalry as Cassidy contends with her high-school nemesis.

Exit Lane by Erika Veurink

A postcollege cross-country road trip sparks *something* between Marin and Teddy—though it's not quite clear what. Over the next eight years, they have fated encounters on multiple continents.

Grape Juice by Eliza Dumais

When Alice lands in France for a wine harvest, she's disenchanted with her life. But she soon finds something she's missing in the vineyard owner's nephew Henri, who's just as lost as she is.

Rooting Interest by Cat Disabato

When Felix gets pulled off her NFL beat to cover the WNBA, she doesn't expect to find herself so taken with the sport—or with one of its biggest stars, Natalie Czapski.

831 STORIES BOOK CREDITS

So many people were involved in bringing this book to life. Many of their names are included here, but there would be no HEA without the passionate work of booksellers and librarians and the enthusiasm of readers. And as we all know, romance readers are the best readers.

831 Stories

Erica Cerulo, Madison Feller, Marie Joh, Catherine Krenzer, Claire Mazur, Elaine Orihuela, Angela Vang

Authors Equity

Andrea Bachofen, Rose Edwards, Carly Gorga, Sarah Christensen Fu, Deb Lewis, Madeline McIntosh, Nina von Moltke, Diana Simmons, Erin Vandeveer, Don Weisberg, Craig Young

C47 Design

Phil Chang, Haneu Kang, Jamin Lee, Naomi Otsu, Sunny Park

Editing

Sanjana Basker, Jen Prokop

Marketing, Events, and Publicity

Emma Benshoff, Tara Larsen, Ashleigh Magee, Kaitlin Phillips, Riley Vaske, Kristin White

Production

Sam Martin, Scribe Inc.

Keep reading for a taste of

Exit Lane

by Erika Veurink

from 831 Stories

I

MARIN

The sun streaks in through the slivers of window on either side of the air-conditioning unit, and it takes me a few waking moments to register the arm of my longtime on-again, off-again girlfriend draped across my chest.

As I gently lift her wrist, Georgie stirs with a devilish smile, bringing me right back to earth. "It's good luck to have sex on graduation day," she hums, kissing my face, my neck, my hip as she shimmies under the covers, armed with the vibrator she left charging the night before. I close my eyes and let my head fall back, trying to be present but feeling far away. Which is actually where I want to be.

When I finish and she comes up for air, I trace a constellation of freckles across her back. "I'll miss this," she says, rolling over into a sunspot on her pilled gray duvet.

"Me too," I say, and I mean it. It's hard to believe I came to the University of Iowa hoping people would think I was straight, worried being bisexual might be some kind of disappointment. But once I settled in—once I got over the novelty of being someone other than the girl with the dead dad—it felt like space opened up for something else. The one-hour-and-fifty-five-minute drive felt far enough away from home to try on an identity that I thought might fit. Self-assured and up-for-anything Georgie, president of Chi Omega, social coordinator of the Pride Alliance Center, helped me find a rhythm, some kind of belonging. But as I kiss her goodbye, I feel a relief, an acknowledgment that my time here is over and that my real life can start.

On campus, parents are at Hy-Vee purchasing black-and-gold "Class of 2017" balloons, cases of Coors, and flimsy greeting cards to stuff with cash. My personal celebration is going to look more like driving a thousand miles and never turning back.

As I step out into the morning sun, rolling my shoulders back into a big stretch, I hear the band tuning its instruments to *Pomp and Circumstance* on the still-dewy turf of Kinnick Stadium. Beneath it, the sound of Sloane's voice as she answers my phone call: "Why are you up?" She responds with a question. Typical. I imagine her filling in the last of the Saturday crossword in pencil while sipping a responsible half cup of coffee. "God, I see you walking from the Chi O house. You think you're so original for getting laid our last morning of college." I wave to where I know my best friend is looking down from the living room we share. She's probably already dressed—like a future First Lady, as usual, a long brown ponytail hanging at the nape of her neck, as carefully constructed as the sculptures at the state fair butter-carving competition.

"Did Teddy confirm what time he could pick me up?" I ask as I cross the street.

"Yep, you're all set to leave at five."

"We can agree he's only doing this because he's desperately in love with you, right?"

She ignores me. "You don't have a car. You're both headed to New York. It just makes sense. But I *can* agree that it is remarkable that he's still willing to do this despite your unwillingness to just text him back directly to coordinate this whole thing. But I am, as ever, happy to act as your admin. I will sort of miss it when you have a real one." Ever logical, she has a way of finishing a sentence that annoys her opponents on the debate team and fills me with calm. She's the one part of my college experience I can't bear to think about leaving. Our plan is to reunite in the city eventually, but for now, we try to avoid the topic of our inevitable distance.

After our freshman year of dorm living, Sloane and I moved into a luxury building on the edge of campus. Though her parents assure me I pay half the rent, we all know my monthly check barely covers the co-op fee.

"Your gown is steamed in the bathroom," she says as soon as I step through the door and kick off my loafers. "There's extra turkey bacon in the oven. And when are you going to deal with your closet? You know, for someone who claims to love a plan . . ."

I reach for her shoulder, smiling, and pull her in for a hug. "I trust that you'll still be micromanaging my life long-distance."

I leave her to her own preparations and collapse, for the last time, onto my bed, a wrought-iron beauty I rescued from Craigslist and transformed with the aid of Sloane and a can of spray paint on the roof during finals. I only ruined one pair of pants.

I look around at everything that's still left to pack. Dad's funeral program tucked into the frame of a pink-and-black *Funny Face* poster. Macroeconomics textbooks I promised my Chi O little. A row of blue and white button-ups, some thrifted blazers. My beloved, pristine loafers, purchased after landing a competitive venture capital internship in New York. My heart rate rises in excitement as I process the gravity of the moment, and I fan my arms like a kid making a snow angel. The back of my throat goes dry, and I'm suddenly lightheaded from anticipation, hunger, or both. Today is the start of the promise I made myself when I was fifteen: that someday I would leave all of Iowa behind. I have two suitcases. Seven hours. And a triple espresso waiting for me in the kitchen.

TEDDY

"Graduation sex"—I barely get the words out, watching Emilie, an ex from freshman year, pulling on a heel at the foot of my bed—"is good sex, I mean, good luck." She smiles, grabs her keys off my dresser, and promises to add me on LinkedIn. I laugh to myself as I tug on my boxers.

After the door shuts, I know it's time to face the

inevitable: I am moving out and moving on, even if a not-insubstantial part of me wishes my life in Iowa City could last forever—the house parties, the group projects I carried mostly on my own, the late nights in the library that turned into early mornings.

When I got accepted into the NYU School of Law, I briefly but seriously considered staying at Iowa instead. After working through a robust pros/cons chart on the whiteboard in my favorite study room in the business school, I knew what I had to do. I'd go learn everything I possibly could from a new place and new people, then bring it all back home. "We'll always be here," my mom reminded me. "Now's the time to spread your wings."

My eyes drift to a stack of cards sitting on top of my dresser: one for my sister Romy, one for my parents, and one for my childhood best friend and forever accomplice, Carter. Notes thanking them for their support the past four years. Proof that learning to shotgun a beer hadn't murdered my manners.

I lean onto my elbow to open the disintegrating blinds, revealing crowds ambling toward the football field. "Amateur hour," I mutter. I'd reserved tickets for my and Carter's families weeks ago and booked an eight-person reservation for late lunch in town. Our combined family dinners used to be a weekly occurrence, most Sunday nights after football games or church, and the weight of this being the last time we'd all be together for a while was palpable. It was a pressure on my chest that kept me from moving to my feet.

I check my phone, fully charged on the windowsill

where I leave it every evening, to find a drunk voicemail I convinced Carter to record for posterity at Donnelly's last night. Nostalgic already, I download it for safekeeping and scroll back to a text from Sloane, confirming plans for me to take someone named Marin with me when I depart for my drive to New York this afternoon. I hadn't planned on company, but how could I say no to the gorgeous, divinely aloof Sloane Bachman?

Three knocks interrupt thoughts of my entirely unrequited crush.

Carter. "Decent!" I shout toward the door, and he enters, balancing two sweating iced coffees in his hands and a bag of bagels under his chin.

"Ran into a very adorable ghost on the way in," he says, dropping the carbs at the foot of my bed with a tilt of his head. "Emilie? From Econ 101?" Carter's encyclopedic memory of my dating life is both endearing and creepy. Plied with enough drinks, he could recite every single one of my love interests since first grade.

I reach for my coffee with an eye roll. "I plead the fifth?"

He laughs. "You ready?"

"One sec." I text Sloane back—promptness equals points in her book—and finally bring my feet to the floor.

The ceremony is eternal, but not long enough. Our parents are waving from row 5, zooming in with their ancient iPhones, dabbing tears. A reminder that the moisture pooling in my own eyes is genetic hardwiring. After lunch, Carter and I both continue to cry in the Joseph's parking lot while our dads pretend to make small talk ten feet away and our moms hover, patting each other's shoulders and digging in their purses for another pack of tissues. Carter is headed to Reno for a top-secret engineering job, and we've spent the last four months trying to pretend like the cross-country moves we're making aren't terrifying. That we have any idea how to navigate the world without each other. We hand each other our letters. "We're so cheesy," Carter jokes, stuffing my note in his pocket. "Obviously I can't read this now. I'm really going to miss you. Promise me you won't fall in love with some Upper East Side snob and never come back?"

I laugh and hug him hard. "It's just for now. We'll get married and have kids, and our kids will get married and have kids, and we'll hardly remember this." I say it in a joking tone, but he knows that I mean it. "Promise to save a spot for me on Fifty-First Street," I add more earnestly.

The plan has always been simple: Carter would live at 441 Fifty-First Street, Des Moines, Iowa, his grandparents' former address and the site of some of our best memories, and I would live in 443 Fifty-First Street next door. But for now, it's Nevada and New York and a shared commitment to call each other every Sunday.

I pull my late grandma's 1998 LeSabre out of the parking lot. The gas light flicks on, and the check engine light follows in short order. It's fine. What matters is getting to the meeting spot on time. In all likelihood, punctuality is Sloane's love language.

When I make the turn in front of the main library, I see them: Sloane, somehow still stoic despite tears streaming down her face, hugging a woman almost a foot taller than her—dark blond, terrifying, with a cigarette dangling from her lip and an *Annie Hall* outfit hanging off her frame. Sloane's in chinos, ballet flats, and a navy-and-white striped boatneck. Are those . . . printed-out directions in her hand? Her friend looks familiar, maybe from an elective or Young Democrats or something. I squint as I approach and pull the visor down.

Now that I have a better view, I can tell that the friend is beautiful—actually, stunning—with features that look like they could slice right through me, though a little too androgynous for my personal taste. Sloane's a gin and tonic after a long day of yard work. This woman—Marin—is a Negroni after a big meeting. *Not that I've ever had a long day of yard work or a big meeting*, I think. She intimidates me even from a distance, and yet her high cheekbones and arched eyebrows make my stomach tighten in a way I recognize. As I roll to a stop at the curb, I sit up straighter, checking for remnants of lunch in my teeth and tracking the way Marin's weight shifts from her front foot to her back, how she lifts her chin while forcing a smile.

The two of them pull apart and walk toward the Buick, where I hand-crank the passenger window open. Sloane turns on a smile, a real one I think, as she angles her stretched-out arms in a sideways V like she's unveiling a work of art. "Teddy, meet Marin."

Sixteen hours. How bad could it be? I reach over to extend a hand out the window.

"Hi, Teddy," she says, eyes narrowing. "Can you open the trunk?"